THE LIBRARY

FROM   OF ·

Puffin Books
Editor: *Kaye Webb*

My Friend Mr Leakey

'Years ago,' Professor Haldane tells us, 'I gave up hanging up a stocking on Christmas Eve. So when I woke up on Christmas morning I was rather surprised to see one of my socks hanging on the bottom of the bed, and much more so when it got up and walked along the counterpane towards me. When it was over my chest it bowed deeply, and emptied out a letter sealed with sealing wax, a turkey's egg, a tie pin with an emerald in it, a fruit which I afterwards found out was a custard apple, and a pocket diary.

Naturally he guessed that the presents were from Mr Leakey, for Mr Leakey was the only magician he knew, the only friend who could bring a sock to life, or bewitch a tie pin and a diary so that he would never lose them.

The letter was an invitation to spend the day after Boxing Day with Mr Leakey, who wanted to run over to Java after lunch, and was going to use a touch of invisibility in the morning to cure a dog that was always biting people. And if you want to know more about Mr Leakey and his household jinn and the octopus who served his meals for him and the dragon (wearing asbestos boots) who grilled the fish, you should read this book to find out.

The illustrations, by Quentin Blake, were made especially for this edition.

For readers of eight and over, especially boys.

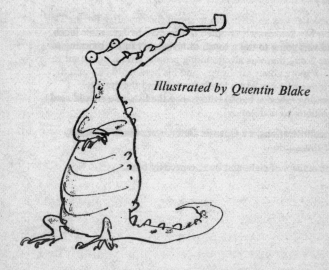

Illustrated by Quentin Blake

J. B. S. Haldane

My Friend Mr Leakey

Penguin Books

Penguin Books Ltd, Harmondsworth,
Middlesex, England
Penguin Books Inc., 7110 Ambassador Road,
Baltimore, Maryland 21207, U.S.A.
Penguin Books Australia Ltd, Ringwood,
Victoria, Australia

First published by The Cresset Press 1937
Published in Puffin Books 1944
Reissued 1971
Reprinted 1972

Made and printed in Great Britain by
Richard Clay (The Chaucer Press) Ltd.,
Bungay, Suffolk
Set in Linotype Times

Contents

A Meal with a Magician

I have had some very odd meals in my time, and if I liked I could tell you about a meal in a mine, or a meal in Moscow, or a meal with a millionaire. But I think you will be more interested to hear about a meal I had one evening with a magician, because it is more unusual. People don't often have a meal of that sort, for rather few people know a magician at all well, because there aren't very many in England. Of course I am talking about real magicians. Some conjurors call themselves magicians, and they are very clever men. But they can't do the sort of things that real magicians do. I mean, a conjuror can turn a rabbit into a bowl of goldfish, but it's always done under cover or behind something, so that you can't see just what is happening. But a real magician can turn a cow into a grandfather clock with people looking on all the time. Only it is very much harder work, and no one could do it twice a day, and six days a week, like the conjurors do with rabbits.

When I first met Mr Leakey I never guessed he was a magician. I met him like this. I was going across the Haymarket about five o'clock one afternoon. When I got to the refuge by a lamp-post in the middle I stopped, but a little man who had crossed so far with me went on. Then he saw a bus going down the hill and jumped back, which is always a silly thing to do. He jumped

9

right in front of a car, and if I hadn't grabbed his over-coat collar and pulled him back on to the refuge, I think the car would have knocked him down. For it was wet weather, and the road was very greasy, so it only skidded when the driver put the brakes on.

The little man was very grateful, but dreadfully frightened, so I gave him my arm across the street, and saw him back to his home, which was quite near. I won't tell you where it was, because if I did you might go there and bother him, and if he got really grumpy it might be very awkward indeed for you. I mean, he might make one of your ears as big as a cabbage-leaf, or turn your hair green, or exchange your right and left feet, or some-thing like that. And then everyone who saw you would burst out laughing, and say, 'Here comes wonky Willie, or lopsided Lizzie,' or whatever your name is.

'I can't bear modern traffic,' he said, 'the motor-buses make me so frightened. If it wasn't for my work in London I should like to live on a little island where there are no roads, or on the top of a mountain, or somewhere like that.' The little man was sure I had saved his life, and insisted on my having dinner with him, so I said I would come to dinner on Wednesday week. I didn't notice anything specially odd about him then, except that his ears were rather large and that he had a little tuft of hair on the top of each of them, rather like the lynx at the Zoo. I remember I thought if I had hair there I would shave it off. He told me that his name was Leakey, and that he lived on the first floor.

Well, on Wednesday week I went to dinner with him. I went upstairs in a block of flats and knocked at a quite

ordinary door, and the little hall of the flat was quite
ordinary too, but when I got inside it was one of the
oddest rooms I have ever seen. Instead of wallpaper
there were curtains round it, embroidered with pictures
of people and animals. There was a picture of two men
building a house, and another of a man with a dog and
a cross-bow hunting rabbits. I know they were made of
embroidery, because I touched them, but it must have
been a very funny sort of embroidery, because the pictures were always changing. As long as you looked at
them they stayed still, but if you looked away and back
again they had altered. During dinner the builders had
put a fresh storey on the house, the hunter had shot a
bird with his cross-bow, and his dog had caught two
rabbits.

The furniture was very funny too. There was a book-
case made out of what looked like glass with the largest
books in it that I ever saw, none of them less than a
foot high, and bound in leather. There were cupboards
running along the tops of the bookshelves. The chairs
were beautifully carved, with high wooden backs, and
there were two tables. One was made of copper, and had
a huge crystal globe on it. The other was a solid lump
of wood about ten feet long, four feet wide, and three
feet high, with holes cut in it so that you could get your
knees under it. There were various odd things hanging
from the ceiling. At first I couldn't make out how the
room was lit. Then I saw that the light came from plants
of a sort I had never seen before, growing in pots. They
had red, yellow, and blue fruits about as big as tomatoes,
which shone. They weren't disguised electric lamps, for

I touched one and it was quite cold, and soft like a fruit.

'Well,' said Mr Leakey, 'what would you like for dinner?'

'Oh, whatever you've got,' I said.

'You can have whatever you like,' he said. 'Please choose a soup.'

So I thought he probably got his dinner from a restaurant, and I said, 'I'll have Bortsch,' which is a red Russian soup with cream in it.

'Right,' he said, 'I'll get it ready. Look here, do you mind if we have dinner served the way mine usually is? You aren't easily frightened, are you?'

'Not very easily,' I said.

'All right, then, I'll call my servant, but I warn you he's rather odd.'

At that Mr Leakey flapped the tops and lobes of his ears against his head. It made a noise like when one claps one's hands, but not so loud. Out of a large copper pot about as big as the copper you wash clothes in, which was standing in one corner, came what at first I thought was a large wet snake. Then I saw it had suckers all down one side, and was really the arm of an octopus. This arm opened a cupboard and pulled out a large towel with which it wiped the next arm that came out. The dry arm then clung on to the wall with its suckers, and gradually the whole beast came out, dried itself, and crawled up the wall. It was the biggest octopus I have ever seen; each arm was about eight feet long, and its body was as big as a sack. It crawled up the wall, and then along the ceiling, holding on by its suckers like a fly. When it got above the table it held on by one arm only, and with the other seven got plates and knives and forks out of the cupboards above the bookshelves and laid the table with them.

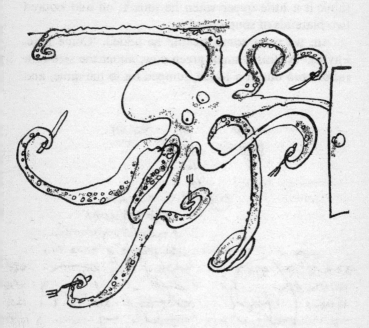

'That's my servant Oliver,' said Mr Leakey. 'He's much better than a person, because he has more arms to work with, and he can hold on to a plate with about ten suckers, so he never drops one.'

When Oliver the octopus had laid the table we sat down and he offered me a choice of water, lemonade, beer, and four different kinds of wine with his seven free arms, each of which held a different bottle. I chose

13

some water and some very good red wine from Burgundy.

All this was so odd that I was not surprised to notice that my host was wearing a top hat, but I certainly did think it a little queer when he took it off and poured two platefuls of soup out of it.

'Ah, we want some cream,' he added. 'Come here, Phyllis.' At this a small green cow, about the size of a rabbit, ran out of a hutch, jumped on to the table, and

stood in front of Mr Leakey, who milked her into a silver cream jug which Oliver had handed down for the purpose. The cream was excellent, and I enjoyed the soup very much.

'What would you like next?' said Mr Leakey.

'I leave it to you,' I answered.

'All right,' he said, 'we'll have grilled turbot, and turkey to follow. Catch us a turbot, please, Oliver, and be ready to grill it, Pompey.'

At this Oliver picked up a fishhook with the end of one of his arms and began making casts in the air like a fly-fisher. Meanwhile I heard a noise in the fireplace, and Pompey came out. He was a small dragon about a foot long, not counting his tail, which measured another foot. He had been lying on the burning coals, and was red-hot. So I was glad to see that as soon as he got out of the fire he put a pair of asbestos boots which were lying in the fender on to his hind feet.

'Now, Pompey,' said Mr Leakey, 'hold your tail up properly. If you burn the carpet again, I'll pour a bucket of cold water over you. (Of course I wouldn't really do that; it's very cruel to pour cold water on to a dragon, especially a little one with a thin skin),' he added in a low voice, which only I could hear. But poor Pompey took the threat quite seriously. He whimpered, and the yellow flames which were coming out of his nose turned a dull blue. He waddled along rather clumsily on his hind legs, holding up his tail and the front part of his body. I think the asbestos boots made walking rather difficult for him, though they saved the carpet, and no doubt kept his hind feet warm. But of course dragons generally walk on all four feet and seldom wear boots, so I was surprised that Pompey walked as well as he did.

I was so busy watching Pompey that I never saw how Oliver caught the turbot, and by the time I looked up at him again he had just finished cleaning it, and threw it down to Pompey. Pompey caught it in his front paws, which had cooled down a bit, and were just about the right temperature for grilling things. He had long thin fingers with claws on the ends; and held the fish on each hand alternately, holding the other against his red-hot chest to warm it. By the time he had finished and put the grilled fish on to a plate which Oliver handed down

Pompey was clearly feeling the cold, for his teeth were chattering, and he scampered back to the fire with evident joy.

'Yes,' said Mr Leakey, 'I know some people say it is cruel to let a young dragon cool down like that, and liable to give it a bad cold. But I say a dragon can't begin to learn too soon that life isn't all fire and flames, and the world is a colder place than he'd like it to be. And they don't get colds if you give them plenty of sulphur to eat. Of course a dragon with a cold is an awful nuisance to itself and everyone else. I've known one throw flames for a hundred yards when it sneezed. But that was a full-grown one, of course. It burned down one of the Emperor of China's palaces. Besides, I really couldn't afford to keep a dragon if I didn't make use of him. Last week, for example, I used his breath to burn the old paint off the door, and his tail makes quite a good soldering iron. Then he's really much more reliable than a dog for dealing with burglars. They might shoot a dog, but leaden bullets just melt the moment they touch Pompey. Anyway, I think dragons were meant for use, not ornament. Don't you?'

'Well, do you know,' I answered, 'I am ashamed to say that Pompey is the first live dragon I've ever seen.'

'Of course,' said Mr Leakey, 'how stupid of me. I have so few guests here except professional colleagues that I forgot you were a layman. By the way,' he went on, as he poured sauce out of his hat over the fish, 'I don't know if you've noticed anything queer about this dinner. Of course some people are more observant than others.'

'Well,' I answered, 'I've never seen anything like it before.'

For example at that moment I was admiring an enormous rainbow-coloured beetle which was crawling towards me over the table with a salt-cellar strapped on its back.

'Ah well then,' said my host, 'perhaps you have guessed that I'm a magician. Pompey, of course, is a real dragon, but most of the other animals here were people before I made them what they are now. Take Oliver, for example. When he was a man he had his legs cut off by a railway train. I couldn't stick them on again because my magic doesn't work against machinery. Poor Oliver was bleeding to death, so I thought the only way to save his life was to turn him into some animal with no legs. Then he wouldn't have any legs to have been cut off. I turned him into a snail, and took him home in my pocket. But whenever I tried to turn him back into something more interesting, like a dog, it had no hind legs. But an octopus has really got no legs. Those eight tentacles grow out of its head. So when I turned him into an octopus, he was all right. And he had been a waiter when he was a man, so he soon learnt his job. I think he's much better than a maid because he can lift the plates from above, and doesn't stand behind one and breathe down one's neck. You may have the rest of the fish, Oliver, and a bottle of beer. I know that's what you like.'

Oliver seized the fish in one of his arms and put it into an immense beak like a parrot's but much bigger, which lay in the centre of the eight arms. Then he took a bottle of beer out of a cupboard, unscrewed the cork with his beak, hoisted himself up to the ceiling with two of his other arms, and turned over so that his mouth was upwards. As he emptied the bottle he winked one of his enormous eyes. Then I felt sure he must be really a man, for I never saw an ordinary octopus wink.

The turkey came in a more ordinary way. Oliver let down a large hot plate, and then a dish cover on to it. There was nothing in the cover, as I could see. Mr Leakey got up, took a large wand out of the umbrella stand, pointed it at the dish cover, said a few words, and there was the turkey steaming hot when Oliver lifted the cover off it.

'Of course that's easy,' said Mr Leakey, 'any good conjuror could do it, but you can never be sure the food you get in that way is absolutely fresh. That's why I like to see my fish caught. But birds are all the better for being a few days old. Ah, we shall want some sausages too. That's easy.'

He took a small clay pipe out of his pocket and blew into it. A large brown bubble came out of the other end, shaped like a sausage. Oliver picked it off with the end of one of his tentacles, and put it on a hot plate, and it was a sausage, because I ate it. He made six sausages in this way, and while I was watching him Oliver had handed down the vegetables. I don't know where he got

19

them. The sauce and gravy came out of Mr Leakey's hat, as usual.

Just after this the only accident of the evening happened. The beetle who carried the salt-cellar round tripped over a fold in the tablecloth and spilled the salt just in front of Mr Leakey, who spoke to him very angrily.

'It's lucky for you, Leopold, that I'm a sensible man. If I were superstitious, which I'm not, I should think I was going to have bad luck. But it's you who are going to have bad luck, if anyone. I've a good mind to turn you back into a man, and if I do, I'll put you straight on to that carpet and send you to the nearest police station; and when the police ask you where you've been hiding, d'you think they'll believe you when you say you've been a beetle for the last year? Are you sorry?'

Leopold, with a great struggle, got out of his harness

and rolled on to his back, feebly waving his legs in the air like a dog does when he's ashamed of himself.

'When Leopold was a man,' said Mr Leakey, 'he made money by swindling people. When the police found it out and were going to arrest him, he came to me for help, but I thought it served him right. So I said 'If they catch you, you'll get sent to penal servitude for seven years. If you like I'll turn you into a beetle for five years, which isn't so long, and then, if you've been a good beetle, I'll make you into a man with a different sort of face, so the police won't know you.' So now Leopold is a beetle. Well, I see he's sorry for spilling the salt. Now, Leopold, you must pick up all the salt you've spilt.'

He turned Leopold over on his front and I watched him begin to pick the salt up. It took him over an hour. First he picked it up a grain at a time in his mouth, lifted himself up on his front legs, and dropped it into the salt-cellar. Then he thought of a better plan. He was a beetle of the kind whose feelers are short and spread out into a fan. He started shovelling the salt with his feelers, and got on much quicker that way. But fairly soon he got uncomfortable. His feelers started to itch or something, and he had to wipe them with his legs. Finally he got a bit of paper, and used it for a shovel, holding it with his front feet.

'That's very clever for a beetle,' said my host. 'When I turn him back into a man he'll be quite good with his hands, and I expect he'll be able to earn his living at an honest job.'

As we were finishing the turkey, Mr Leakey looked up anxiously from time to time.

'I hope Abdu'l Makkar won't be late with the strawberries,' he said.

'Strawberries?' I asked in amazement, for it was the middle of January.

'Oh yes, I've sent Abdu'l Makkar, who is a jinn, to New Zealand for some. Of course it's summer there. He oughtn't to be long now, if he has been good, but you know what jinns are, they have their faults, like the rest of us; curiosity, especially. When one sends them on long errands they will fly too high. They like to get up quite close to Heaven to overhear what the angels are saying, and then the angels throw shooting stars at them. Then they drop their parcels, or come home half scorched. He ought to be back soon, he's been away over an hour. Meanwhile we'll have some other fruit, in case he's late.'

He got up, and tapped the four corners of the table with his wand. At each corner the wood swelled; then it cracked, and a little green shoot came out and started growing. In a minute they were already about a foot high, with several leaves at the top, and the bottom quite woody. I could see from the leaves that one was a cherry, another a pear, and the third a peach, but I didn't know the fourth.

As Oliver was clearing away the remains of the turkey with four of his arms and helping himself to a sausage with a fifth, Abdu'l Makkar came in. He came feet first through the ceiling, which seemed to close behind him like water in the tank of the diving birds'

house in the Zoo, when you look at it from underneath while a penguin dives in. It shook a little for a moment afterwards. He narrowly missed one of Oliver's arms, but alighted safely on the floor, bending his knees to break his fall, and bowing deeply to Mr Leakey. He had a brown face with rather a long nose, and looked quite like a man, except that he had a pair of leathery wings folded on his back, and his nails were of gold. He wore a turban and clothes of green silk.

'O peacock of the world and redresser of injustices,' he said, 'thy unworthy servant comes into the presence with rare and refreshing fruit.'

'The presence deigns to express gratification at the result of thy labours.'

23

'The joy of thy negligible slave is as the joy of King Solomon, son of David (on whom be peace, if he has not already obtained peace) when he first beheld Balkis, the queen of Sheba. May the Terminator of Delights and Separator of Companions be far from this dwelling.'

'May the Deluder of Intelligences never trouble the profundity of thine apprehension.'

'O dominator of demons and governor of goblins, what egregious enchanter or noble necromancer graces thy board?'

'It is written, O Abdu'l Makkar, in the book of the sayings of the prophet Shoaib, the apostle of the Midianites, that curiosity slew the cat of Pharaoh, king of Egypt.'

'That is a true word.'

'Thy departure is permitted. Awaken me at the accustomed hour. But stay! My safety razor hath no more blades and the shops of London are closed. Fly therefore to Montreal, where it is even now high noon, and purchase me a packet thereof.'

'I tremble and obey.'

'Why dost thou tremble, O audacious among the Ifreets?'

'O Emperor of enchantment, the lower air is full of aeroplanes, flying swifter than a magic carpet,* and each making a din like unto the bursting of the great dam of Sheba, and the upper air is infested with meteorites.'

'Fly therefore at a height of five miles and thou shalt avoid both the one peril and the other. And now, O

* This is of course a gross exaggeration.

24

performer of commands and executor of behests, thou hast my leave to depart.'

'May the wisdom of Plato, the longevity of Shiqq, the wealth of Solomon, and the success of Alexander, be thine.'

'The like unto thee, with brazen knobs thereon.'

The jinn now vanished, this time through the floor. While he and Mr Leakey had been talking the trees had grown up to about four feet high, and flowered. The flowers were now falling off, and little green fruits were swelling.

'You have to talk like that to a jinn or you lose his respect. I hope you don't mind my not introducing you, but really jinns may be quite awkward at times,' said my host. 'Of course Abdu'l Makkar is a nice chap and means well, but he might be very embarrassing to you, as you don't know the Word of Power to send him away. For instance if you were playing cricket and went in against a fast bowler, he'd probably turn up and ask you "Shall I slay thine enemy, O Defender of the Stumps, or merely convert him into an he-goat of loathsome appearance and afflicted with the mange?" You know, I used to be very fond of watching cricket, but I can't do it now. Quite a little magic will upset a match. Last year I went to see the Australians playing against Gloucester, and just because I felt a little sympathetic with Gloucestershire the Australian wickets went down like ninepins. If I hadn't left before the end they'd have been beaten. And after that I couldn't go to any of the test matches. After all, one wants the best side to win.'

We next ate the New Zealand strawberries, which

were very good, with Phyllis's cream. While we did so Pompey, who acted as a sort of walking stove, came out again and melted some cheese to make a Welsh rarebit. After this we went on to dessert. The fruit was now quite ripe. The fourth tree bore half a dozen beautiful golden fruits shaped rather like apricots, but much bigger, and my host told me they were mangoes, which of course usually grow in India. In fact you can't make them grow in England except by magic. So I said I would try a mango.

'Aha,' said Mr Leakey, 'this is where I have a pull over Lord Melchett or the Duke of Westminster, or any other rich man. They might be able to get mangoes here by aeroplane, but they couldn't give them as dessert at a smart dinner-party.'

'Why not?' I asked.

'That shows you've never eaten one. The only proper place to eat a mango is in your bath. You see, it has a tough skin and a squashy inside, so when once you get through the skin all the juice squirts out. And that would make a nasty mess of people's white shirts. D'you ever wear a stiff-fronted shirt?'

'Not often.'

'A good thing too. You probably don't know why people wear them. It's a curious story. About a hundred years ago a great Mexican enchanter called Whizto-pacoatl came over to Europe. And he got very annoyed with the rich men. He didn't so much mind their being rich, but he thought they spent their money on such ugly things, and were dreadfully stodgy and smug. So he decided to turn them all into turtles. Now to do that

somebody has to say two different spells at the same time, which is pretty difficult, I can tell you. So Whizto-pacoatl went round to an English sorcerer called Mr Benedict Barnacle, to borrow a two-headed parrot that belonged to him. It was rather like one of those two-headed eagles they used to have on the Russian and

Austrian flags. Then he was going to teach one of the heads one spell, and the other head the second spell; and when the parrot said both at once all the rich men would have turned into turtles. But Mr Barnacle persuaded him to be less fierce, so finally they agreed that for a hundred years the rich men in Europe should be made to wear clothes only fit for turtles. Because of course the front of a turtle is stiff and flat, and it is the only sort of animal that would be quite comfortable in a shirt with a stiff flat front. They made a spell to stiffen all the shirts, and of course it worked very well, but it's wearing off now, and soon nobody will wear such silly clothes any more.

'About your mango; you can eat it quite safely, if you just wait a moment while I enchant it so that it won't splash over you.'

Quite a short spell and a little wiggling of his wand were enough, and then I ate the mango. It was wonderful. It was the only fruit I have ever eaten that was better than the best strawberries. I can't describe the flavour, which is a mixture of all sorts of things, including a little resin, like the smell of a pine forest in summer. There is a huge flattish stone in the middle, too big to get into your mouth, and all round it a squashy yellow pulp. To test the spell I tried to spill some down my waistcoat, but it merely jumped up into my mouth. Mr Leakey ate a pear, and gave me the other five mangoes to take home. But I had to eat them in my bath because they weren't enchanted.

While we were having coffee (out of the hat, of course) Mr Leakey rubbed one corner of the table with his wand and it began to sprout with very fine green grass. When it was about as high as the grass on a lawn, he called Phyllis out of her hutch, and she ate some of it for her dinner. We talked for a while about magic, football, and the odder sorts of dog, such as Bedlington terriers and rough-haired dachshunds, and then I said I must be getting home.

'I'll take you home,' said Mr Leakey, 'but when you have a day to spare you must come round and spend it with me, if you'd care to see the sort of things I generally do, and we might go over to India or Java or somewhere for the afternoon. Let me know when you're free. But now just stand on this carpet, and shut your eyes, because people often get giddy the first two or three times they travel by magic carpet.'

We got on to the carpet. I took a last look at the table, where Leopold had just finished picking up the salt, and was resting, while Phyllis was chewing the cud. Then I shut my eyes, my host told the carpet my address, flapped his ears, and I felt a rush of cold air on my cheeks, and a slight giddiness. Then the air was warm again. Mr Leakey told me to open my eyes, and I was in my sitting-room at home, five miles away. As the room is small, and there were a number of books and things on the floor, the carpet could not settle down properly and stayed about a foot up in the air. Luckily it was quite stiff, so I stepped down off it, and turned the light on.

'Good night,' said Mr Leakey, bending down to shake my hand, and then he flapped his ears and he and the carpet vanished. I was left in my room with nothing but

29

a nice full feeling and a parcel of mangoes to persuade me that I had not been dreaming.

If you like this story I will tell you later on about a day I spent with Mr Leakey helping him with his work, and how Pompey was naughty and ran away down a volcano. But that is quite a different story. Still, I hope you think my friend Mr Leakey is a nice man. Because I do.

A Day in the Life
of a Magician

I told you before about a dinner I had one evening with my friend Mr Leakey, a magician who lives in London. Before I left him I promised to spend a day with him some time, and now I am going to tell you about that day.

Years ago I gave up hanging up a stocking on Christmas Eve. One reason is that I have no stockings to hang, because I almost always wear trousers, and even when I wear shorts I wear socks with them so as to make my calves brown. And I don't think Father Christmas would find room in a sock for all the things I want. So when I woke up on Christmas morning I was rather surprised to see one of my socks hanging on the bottom of the bed, and much more so when it got up and walked along the counterpane towards me. When it was over my chest it bowed deeply, and emptied out a letter sealed with sealing wax, a turkey's egg, a tie pin with an emerald in it, a fruit which I afterwards found out was a custard apple, and a pocket diary. I guessed at once that the presents were from Mr Leakey, because none of my other friends would have been able to send me things in that way. And when I opened the letter I found that it was an invitation to spend the day after Boxing Day with him. Besides this he told me what the egg and fruit were, and that the tie pin and diary had been bewitched so that I could not lose them, which is what I generally do with pins and diaries.

The day after Boxing Day I went round to Mr Leakey's flat after breakfast. This time the door was opened by Abdu'l Makkar, Mr Leakey's jinn. He was dressed as a footman, with brass buttons, and took my coat and hat to hang them up. The only odd thing about it was that he stood about two feet away and never touched my coat when he was taking it off. It felt rather queer, but I was accustomed to queer feelings in that house.

Mr Leakey greeted me warmly when I went into his room. So did Pompey the dragon, who was sitting on the fire. He started flapping his wings when I came in, which made the fire smoke, but Mr Leakey had only to pick up a magic wand which was lying on the table, and Pompey at once lay down quietly with his head between his paws.

'I thought we might go over to Java for lunch,' said my host, 'but there are a couple of things I want to do this morning. Would you like to come round with me? If not stay here and smoke a pipe, and I'll arrange an entertainment for you.'

'I'll come out with you, if you're sure I shan't be in the way,' I answered.

'Oh no, I shall be delighted to have you with me, but you may have to become invisible, so you'd better practise here, because it feels rather funny the first time. Put this cap of darkness on, and walk round the room once or twice. If you look down you may feel giddy. So if you find you're losing your balance look straight in front of you.'

He handed me a black cap with a peak to it, about the shape of the paper hats you get out of a Christmas cracker. It was the blackest thing I have ever seen, not a bit the colour of ordinary black cloth or paper, but like the colour of a black hole. You could not see what it was made of, or whether it was smooth or rough. It didn't feel like cloth or anything ordinary, but like very soft warm india-rubber. I put it on, and at once my arm

35

disappeared. Everything looked slightly odd, and at first I couldn't think why. Then I saw that the two ghostly noses which I always see without noticing them were gone. I shut one of my eyes, as one does if one wants to see one's nose more clearly. I felt my eye shut, but it made no difference. Of course now that I was invisible my eyelids and nose were quite transparent! Then I looked to where my body and legs ought to have been, but of course I saw nothing. I got a horrid giddy feeling and had to catch hold of the table with an invisible hand. However I steadied myself and looked straight in front of me, and quite soon I was able to walk round the room easily enough.

'Put the cap in your pocket when we go out,' said my host. 'Then when you want to be invisible, put it on under your hat. It will make that invisible all right, just like it does your clothes.'

We went out into the street. This time no one was there in the hall, but my hat and coat just flew off their pegs and put themselves on to me.

'First,' said Mr Leakey as we got into a taxi, 'I'm going to deal with a dog who is making a nuisance of himself. He bites people, and unless I do something about it the police will have him killed. But I'm going to do something about it. Then I'm going to make a cheque invisible, and perhaps one or two other little things. Of course one can't do magic on a big scale in London. It would attract notice, and people would start worrying me, which I don't like. But I like to be useful in a small way. For example I think our taxi-driver would look better without all those spots. Don't you?'

Certainly the driver had pimples enough on his face to make an advertisement for one of those wonderful medicines you read about in the newspapers. Mr Leakey took up his umbrella, which had such a queer handle that I guessed at once that it must really be a magic wand, and started twirling it about. Through the front window of the taxi I could see two large pimples on the driver's neck suddenly fading away, and by the time we got to the address he had been given, his face was as smooth as a tomato, though he never seemed to notice anything happening.

Mr Leakey gave him a coin. '' 'Ere, guvnor, you've given me a farthing,' said the driver.

'Look again.'

'Well, I'm –, 'aven't seen one of them since 1914.'

'Of course,' said Mr Leakey to me, as we walked away, 'I've got a magic purse, but you can only get gold out of it, not notes, because magic purses were invented long before printing. It's a nuisance. Before the first world war one could sometimes pay in gold, and no one was surprised, but now most people have never seen a real golden sovereign, or half a sovereign, which is what I gave the driver. Well, there aren't many people about; I think you might put your cap on. Of course it doesn't do to be invisible in a crowd. People bump into you, and get terribly frightened.'

I put my cap on and vanished. Mr Leakey pointed his magic umbrella at himself, and suddenly both he and the umbrella disappeared, except for the very tip of the umbrella, which seemed to go on walking along the street in a series of hops like a bird.

'Now,' he said, 'come after me into this garden, and
see me deal with the dog. Shut the gate behind you.
Don't stop him if he tries to bite either of us. He won't.'

As I shut the gate a large mongrel dog ran towards
us growling. He had an angry but puzzled look, and
soon stopped growling to sniff. Suddenly he seemed to
make up his mind. I think most dogs except greyhounds
pay more attention to smells than to what they see.
Anyway this dog suddenly ran towards Mr Leakey. I
could see where he was, because the end of his magic
umbrella was visible. As the dog ran towards him, the
end was lifted up, and a tiny puff of purplish smoke
came out of it. The dog did not stop, but suddenly
looked even more puzzled than before. Then Mr
Leakey's left leg became visible from the knee downwards, and very odd it looked. The dog at last saw something to bite, and rushed at the leg snarling. Mr Leakey,

or at least his left leg, stood quite still, and before I
could stop him, the dog bit it. You know how a dog
pulls his lips back when he is angry, so that you can see
all his teeth. I could see that this dog had a very fine
set. But when he bit Mr Leakey's trouser the teeth didn't

go through it. They just bent. 'I've turned them into white india-rubber,' he said, 'all except four molars at the back. They'll be all right for grinding up dog biscuits. Ah, here's his master. I think I'll hide my leg again.' As the dog's owner, a very grumpy-looking man, came out, the leg vanished, but clearly Mr Leakey lifted it up, for he swung the dog up into the air, where he stayed for a time. I never saw a dog looking so funny. He hung in the air with his mouth wide open and all his teeth bent sideways. Then suddenly he dropped off, and went away with his tail between his legs.

The grumpy man stood stock still with his legs wide apart and his mouth opened in amazement. He hardly opened it any wider when he saw the handle of his garden gate turn, and the gate open and shut again behind us as we went out. When we went round the street corner we became visible again, which was rather a relief to me, because it is certainly odd to feel bits of oneself without seeing them. As we got into another taxi Mr Leakey said, 'If that man had any sense, which he hasn't, he'd make a fortune by showing Fido at fairs as The Rubber-toothed Dog, and charging people sixpence to let him bite them.' By the way, if anyone who reads this does see a rubber-toothed dog at a fair, I wish they'd write to me, because I should like to meet Fido again, and see if he's got accustomed to his rubber teeth, like people get accustomed to false ones.

'I expect you wonder how I can turn things into rubber by magic, because it's rather a new sort of stuff in Europe, and we haven't got spells that will work on new sorts of stuff like aluminium or stainless steel, or aspirin or artificial silk. I learned the trick from a Brazilian magician who was at the International Congress of Sorcerers on the Brocken in Germany in 1912. I taught him some magic about iron and steel, and he showed me how to turn teeth into rubber. They find it very useful there with jaguars and crocodiles and anacondas. Of course rubber trees grow there naturally, so the magicians know all about rubber. Now we're going to visit a moneylender who calls himself Mr Macstewart. Of course that isn't his real name. His real name's quite horrid, full of Z's. You can't touch people with some sorts of magic unless you know their real names. That's why moneylenders always have false names, to protect themselves against good magicians who would like to turn them into sausages or door handles or foot-scrapers or armchairs or something useful. It's very important to hide your real name if you have anything to do with magic, and of course compound interest is one of the very blackest sorts of magic. No one knows my real name, any more than they know the real name of London. It has a secret name which only the Lord Mayor knows, and he tells it to the new Lord Mayor each year. If a bad magician found out its real name he would be able to turn it into Stow-on-the-Wold or Ballybunnion or Timbuctoo or Omborombonga, which would be very awkward.

'Princes and kings have such a lot of names because it makes it harder to bewitch them. Of course if you enchant anyone you generally have to say their full name, pronouncing all the bits of it properly, and you have to get that and the spell into one breath. That's why kings and emperors have names like Augustus Benhadad Charlemagne Dagobert Ethelwulf Frederick Genseric Hardicanute Ixtlilcochitl Jehoiakim Kamehameha Leonidas Maximilian Napoleon Obadiah Polycrates Quirinus Rehoboam Subiluliuma Tarassicodissa Umsilikazi Valentinian Wenceslaus Xerxes Yoshihito Zedekiah the hundred and seventeenth.* You haven't much breath left for a spell when you've said that, especially if you pronounce Ixtlilcochitl and the first X in Xerxes properly.

'Well, here we are. Mr Macstewart is being rather a nuisance to all sorts of poor people, and some of them have promised to pay him back two or three times what he lent them first. I've warned him about it, and he's rather annoyed with me, so I'm going to be invisible. But really it looks so funny when an invisible man opens several doors that I think it would be best if you stayed visible and I kept close behind you. I'm not going to turn him into a sausage this time, only to make a few signatures invisible, so that he won't be able to make people pay him money.'

We got out at a rather grand office with glass doors. Mr Leakey became invisible half-way upstairs. I said

* By the way, you mayn't know some of these kings' names. Dagobert was king of France. He was a good king, but he wore his trousers back to front. Ixtlilcochitl was king of Texcuca in Mexico, and an ally of Cortez. Several Kamehamehas were kings of Hawaii. Subiluliuma was king of the Hittites. Tarassicodissa became emperor of Constantinople, but they made him change his name, which was Isaurian, so he called himself Zeno. Umsilikazi was king of the Matabeles in South Africa. Some people called him Moselikatze, and others Silkaats. All the rest come in history books or the Bible.

41

I wanted to borrow £1000, and I was shown in to Mr Macstewart. I went very slowly through the doors so that Mr Leakey could follow me easily. I didn't really like Mr Macstewart. He wasn't the sort of man I would borrow money from even if there was no hurry about paying back, and no compound, or even simple, interest. When I want to borrow money I always go to a friend called Dr Barnet Woolf, who thinks it is wicked to pay interest for it. I owe him twopence halfpenny at present.

While I was talking to Mr Macstewart about borrowing £1000, I noticed the end of the umbrella moving about in the air. Mr Leakey was pointing it at all sorts of bits of paper to make the ink on them invisible. I saw Mr Macstewart looking at it out of the corner of his eye, but he didn't say anything. I expect he thought that if he talked about it I should say he was mad. After about three minutes the end of the umbrella went down on to the floor, and I told Mr Macstewart that he wanted more interest than I could pay on the £1000. So out I went, and the end of the umbrella close behind me. Just as I was opening the door it went up into the air and wiggled quickly. It left behind it a track of pink light like the neon tubes in advertisements. This was a bit of writing, which I read from behind, because the front of it was towards Mr Macstewart. But I could read it all right, like one can read the writing on shop windows from inside. What I read was:

SAUSAGE NEXT TIME

Mr Macstewart went all goggle-eyed, and although his hair was very greasy it stood up on end like a clothes brush, and he began to perspire all over his face.

'I hope there won't have to be a next time,' said Mr Leakey, as we got into a third taxi; 'people like that are generally easy to frighten, and I'm not asking him to give up his job, only to be a bit less unkind about it. Well, that's all the work I'm going to do today. Where shall we go for lunch? I think Java would be nice. Oh no, it's too late, the sun's setting there now, and it will be dark before we get there. Let's go somewhere in India. Mandu would be all right at this time of year. We'll go by carpet. You'll want a parachute in case you falls off on the way, amulets to protect you against jinns and Rakshasas, and pyrethrum oil to keep off mosquitoes. Also some cool clothes. You won't need a sun-helmet, it's three o'clock in the afternoon there, but it will be fairly warm after London.'

There was a great bustle in the house when we got back there about eleven o'clock. All sorts of magic things were happening. Cupboard doors were opening, and clothes, amulets, magic wands, books of spells, and what not, were jumping out and packing themselves into a hamper. When the hamper was full it shut itself, and a snake came out of another basket and wriggled its head underneath. It did this twice altogether, so that the hamper was done up like a parcel with string, and finally it tied its head and tail together on the top into a nice loop. 'Clementina saves me a lot of money for string,' said Mr Leakey, 'and she sees the world like this, besides protecting my hamper in case anyone

wanted to steal it. We shall be flying fairly high, so I
shall have to do some magic on you. When we get about
five miles up the air gets very thin, and you'll want
more blood, and several other things too, to live up
there. I might give you an oxygen breathing apparatus
like an airman, but I shouldn't know what to do if it
went wrong. I don't care for all this machinery; there's
nothing like good old-fashioned magic. If I give you a
potion it will take about half an hour to work, so the
easiest thing will be to unscrew a bit of you and put the
stuff straight in. Sit down here and put your left leg on
this stool, and I'll unscrew your foot. Volume three of
Hermes Trismegistus, please, Oliver.'

Oliver the octopus, who had been sitting quietly in
his copper cauldron all this time, suddenly shot out two
arms, took his towel in one, dried the end of the other,
and handed down a perfectly enormous book about two
feet long and one across, from the bookshelf. Mr
Leakey turned over the pages and read out a spell. Then
he took my left foot, shoe and all, and unscrewed it.
It didn't hurt a bit, though it felt funny. It unscrewed
just above the ankle. It didn't bleed at all, and I could
see the two bones as he took the foot off. He took a
golden thing like a motor tyre pump and squirted something out of it into the stump of my leg. I felt a nice
warm feeling going up my leg into me. Then he screwed
my foot on again. I could still see the join, but he said
another spell, and my leg looked just as it had done
before.

Abdu'l Makkar now came in. This time he was
dressed like a jinn in a turban and green silk robes, and

you could see his wings, which had been in his coat-tails before.

'He looks better like that, but when he's opening the door to ordinary people I like him to put his wings inside the tails of his coat so as not to frighten them. Of course tail coats come from Persia. People only began to wear them here in King Charles II's time. They were invented by King Nushirvan of Persia, who had a lot of jinns at his court, mostly with wings. He was a very just man, and believed in equality for everyone but himself. He didn't want to make distinctions between jinns and men, so he had to invent a costume that would suit both. Later on the jinns went off, because his magic ring was stolen, but the men in Persia went on wearing tail coats.'

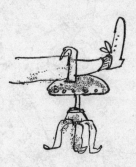

'O sovereign of sorcerers,' said Abdu'l Makkar, bowing deeply, 'thine unworthy and abject slave Pompey craveth a boon.'

'What boon, O swifter than the swallows?'

'He desireth to accompany us on our journey, and promiseth that his conduct shall be as blameless as the conduct of the camel of the Prophet, on whom be peace.'

'Verily since Saturday the feast of St Lucy, when he burned my sausages, his conduct hath been blameless. His request is granted, and his desire shall be satisfied. Bring therefore a brazier whereon he may sit, and place it upon the carpet, with a mat of asbestos beneath. Equip my guest with a parachute and a lifebelt, the first lest he fall from the carpet through the air, the second lest he descend thence into the ocean.'

I put on the parachute and the lifebelt, and also took a magic wand which was handed to me. I felt like one of the soldiers in the battle of the Canal du Nord in September 1918, when two British divisions attacked the Germans in lifebelts, because they had to get across the canal. Abdu'l Makkar came in with a large carpet rolled up, and unrolled about half of it. It was covered with very odd patterns, and had some Arabic words on it. There was no room to unroll the rest. We got on to it, and Abdu'l Makkar lifted up the hamper by the loop in Clementina, and put it down beside us, along with a number of cushions. Then he brought in from another room a brazier full of red-hot coke like night watch-men have to keep them warm. I noticed that he took hold of the red-hot iron with his bare hands, but of course everyone knows that is one of the things jinns can do without being hurt. Pompey flew out of the fireplace and coiled himself up comfortably on top of the coke. The rest of us sat down on the cushions.

'Shut your eyes or you may be giddy when we start,' said Mr Leakey. I did. Then I heard him flap his ears, and felt the carpet rise. I don't know how we got through the ceiling, but it felt rather nasty. I felt us rising very quickly. Then we seemed to be falling, but I clenched my teeth and hoped for the best. When I was told to open my eyes again the sun was shining brightly, though it had been cloudy in London. I crawled to the edge of the carpet, which had now unrolled, and looked over, but saw nothing but a sea of clouds below me. We

47

were moving over them south-eastwards at an enormous rate, but I felt no wind.

'Of course the air round a magic carpet moves with it or we'd be blown off, and I've got a special charm to keep it warm,' explained my host. Through a gap in the clouds I saw the English Channel for a few seconds, and then we were over France. We passed Paris on our left. I could just see the Eiffel tower and the Sacré Coeur church. Then we came over some more clouds, and the next thing I noticed were the Alps ahead of us and mostly rather to the left. We crossed them without trouble, for we were more than two miles above Mont Blanc, and flew over north Italy and then down the Adriatic sea. About ten minutes after starting we were crossing southern Greece, where there were some fairly big mountains. The sun was already much higher in the sky. As we were crossing the Mediterranean, which was a beautiful blue compared with the English Channel, Mr Leakey put an amulet round my neck.

'By the way,' he said, 'we may possibly have a little trouble in the next ten minutes. You remember King Solomon shut up a lot of wicked jinns in bottles, and threw them into the sea. Well, now they're making a big new harbour at Haifa, on the coast of Palestine, and they keep on dredging up these bottles. Every now and then some idiot opens one and the jinn gets out. Well, of course they're very angry. So would you be if you'd been shut up without room to turn round for nearly three thousand years. I think Solomon might have put them in larger bottles myself. They get out and fly about in the air. But the air isn't what it was for jinns. The radio waves go right through them and give them pains in the stomach, which makes them still angrier. Poor Abdu'l Makkar used to have an awful time of it when they first started broadcasting. So I went round to a friend of mine who's a physicist, and he made him a little gadget which protects him all right. But I believe when he's flying very quick he interferes with the receiving sets underneath, and people say it's an atmospheric.

'Well, as I was saying, these jinns get very grumpy and sometimes attack harmless travellers like me. Of course they daren't come near Europe. Too much radio. This amulet will protect you, though. It's got the Sura't al Muwidhettani, the last two chapters of the Koran, on it. If you see a jinn, point your wand at him and recite them. Dear me, don't you know them, where were you at school? In my trade you have to belong to at least eight religions, so as to know how to deal with different sorts of spirits, but lots of people seem only to belong to one, or even none at all. I should be quite afraid of Rakshasas if I weren't a good Hindu, and when I go to China the Great Green Jade Toad might stamp on my chest if I weren't a Taoist. As for Tibet, well I ask you. Would you like to go there if you weren't a Mahayana Buddhist? It's crawling with demons as black as your hat, with teeth like sharks and claws like eagles. Well, you'd better recite the dates of the Kings of England, that will be nearly as good. Don't worry about Egbert, you can begin with William the Conqueror.'

By this time we were over the right-hand bottom corner of the Mediterranean on the map. We could see a lot of ships going into and out of the Suez Canal, which we left on our right, and went on over Mount Sinai, which looked very barren, but not as high as I expected. The sun was now quite hot. I couldn't take off my coat, because of the amulet, lifebelt, and parachute, but Mr Leakey kindly turned my woollen vest and pants into silk with a single twist of his wand, which helped things. Soon we were flying over Arabia. At first there were a lot of green patches, but afterwards we saw nothing below us but great waves of red sand, with very occasionally a few palm trees round a well.

Then in front of us appeared a dull brown patch, hiding the desert beneath it. 'Sandstorm,' said Mr Leakey, ''Ware jinn.' As we came over the sandstorm something like a thundercloud suddenly rose ahead of us. As we looked it shaped into a huge face with a mouth about half a mile across. Mr Leakey simply pointed his wand at it, and it bobbed down.

'Look out astern,' said he, as we passed over the jinn. Sure enough, as soon as we had passed he bobbed up again. 'I'm busy,' said Mr Leakey. I dared not turn round to look what was happening, though I felt the carpet swerve out of its course. The jinn was now rushing at us like an enormous black cloud. I could see into his mouth, which was all fiery inside. He was nearly, but not quite, as alarming as a creeping barrage. That came at one like a black cloud full of flashes of fire, but it was nastier because of the awful noise it made. The jinn was probably making quite a horrid noise, but of course we couldn't hear it, because the carpet was travelling much faster than sound.

I pointed my wand at him, and started on William

51

the Conqueror. The jinn immediately looked uncomfortable, and his face got much smaller, only about as big as a house. I could see his body too. It was a nasty greyish-green colour. Still he came on after us. I had an awkward moment when I hesitated over the date of Henry III, and saw his face swelling again, but I got it right and he became smaller once more. Clearly he didn't dare to come nearer than about a hundred yards from us. He made some very nasty grimaces, and breathed out fire, but this blew back in his face because he was flying so fast; about three miles a second, I should judge. When I had got to William and Mary, and was beginning to wonder whether one began again after 'George V, 1910', Mr Leakey turned round with a wand in each hand. 'I've dealt with the others in front. Abdu'l Makkar can keep a look out.' As he said this something like a lasso of violet flame flew out of one of the wands and caught the jinn round the neck. I felt the lurch as Mr Leakey braced his feet against two loops in the carpet and started hauling the jinn in like a fisherman with a salmon. He pointed the other wand at the jinn, who wriggled horribly and got quite small. When his whole body was only about twenty feet long Mr Leakey said, 'Bite his nose off, Pompey.' Pompey flew off his nest, landed with all four feet on the jinn's face, and bit his nose off. He flew back licking his lips and wagging his tail, and sat down again on the fire.

Mr Leakey let go the jinn, who stopped flying, and vanished in the distance behind us in an instant. 'That'll teach him to interfere with traffic,' said he. 'I dealt with two others in front all right. Ah, here's a fourth.' I saw a monstrous purple face with huge tusks on our left, but suddenly it was screwed up as if with pain, and vanished. 'Ah ha! we shan't be worried by those chaps any more on this trip. That was the beam wireless from Rugby to Australia with a message about the prices of Portland cement and spelter (whatever that is). It got our purple-faced friend fair and square in the stomach and knocked all the wind out of him. We're off the main force of the beam. It goes over Persia, and keeps it pretty clear of jinns. But even here it's nasty for them. I think you can put your wand down. I hope you didn't mind our little adventure. I should find life very dull without something of that kind at least once a month.'

'Well, I was rather frightened, I must admit. You see, I'd never seen any jinns before except our friend here.'

'The testimony of thy friendship is as precious to my soul as was the manna in the wilderness to the children of Israel,' said Abdu'l Makkar.

'The friendship of so gifted an Ifreet is more valuable to me than was the gold of Ophir unto King Solomon, on whom be peace,' I answered. It is not so hard as it sounds to talk like that. 'I'm glad you're learning the art of polite conversation with supernatural beings,' said Mr Leakey. 'Of course *we* weren't in any danger, but those jinns might have been rather awkward for a beginner. I'm afraid we've got a bit out of our course, though, in manoeuvring for position. That's the Persian Gulf below you. I think we'll go somewhere in northern India instead of Mandu. What about Delhi?'

We flew along for a minute or two over the south coast of Persia and Baluchistan. I saw a few ships, and

two aeroplanes on the route between India and Baghdad. Of course they were far below us, and we were
going so quick that they seemed to be standing quite
still. We passed the mouth of the Indus and Karachi,
and then went inland over another desert. Soon after we
came to the end of the desert I felt the carpet slowing
down and saw a great river in front of us which I guessed
was the Jumma, and a city with a huge red dome and four
white towers round it. Beyond the city lay more big red
and white buildings in gardens, and farther still an
enormous stone tower and a wonderful blue dome. The
carpet now dropped, which gave me a horrid feeling.
You may think you know it from going down in a lift,
but you don't unless you have been down a fairly deep
mine. One feels that one has left all one's inside behind.
The feeling only lasts a second or so in a mine, but this
time it went on longer. Then I felt as if we were rising
again, which of course only means that the fall is slowing down. I looked over the edge, and saw a lot of
people in the streets, but none of them were looking up.
They didn't seem to notice us. 'They can't see us,' said
Mr Leakey. 'Magic carpets are invisible from below
when they're flying. Otherwise those jinns would have
attacked us from underneath. Of course a lot of animals
try to be invisible by having white bellies. Most fish, for
example. But you can't really be invisible except by
magic. Now we're going to call on my friend Mr Chandrajotish, who is a sorcerer, and a very good one too.'

The carpet came down in a beautiful little garden with
fountains and orange trees, with a white marble colon-
nade round it. We got off the carpet, and Abdu'l Makkar

lifted Pompey and the hamper off it. The carpet then rolled itself up, and stood in a corner. Two most lovely ladies came out, one with an oval brown face, the other rather yellower, with slightly slanting eyes, and a golden filigree pendant set with rubies hanging from her nose.

'Mrs Sitabai Chandrajotish and Mrs Radhika Chandrajotish,' said Mr Leakey, and started talking to them in Urdu, too quickly for me to follow, though I gathered that Mr Chandrajotish was away. A third Mrs Chandrajotish now appeared, for of course Indians are allowed to marry quite a lot of wives if they want to. She had a rather paler face and from her long pointed ears I guessed she was a jinniyah, in fact the first lady jinn I had ever seen. She picked Pompey up, although he was red-hot, and put him in her lap. Then she made him sit up and beg for little lumps of sulphur and red-hot bits of some stuff or other. I don't know enough about dragons to say what it was. Mr Leakey had to ask her to stop. 'I don't like to see dragons too fat,' he said to me. 'A dragon ought to be thin like a dachshund. Of course different breeds differ. European dragons aren't so very slim, but you ought to be able to tie four knots in a good specimen of a Chinese dragon, just as you can tie one in a well-bred giraffe's neck. If ever you think of breeding giraffes for amusement remember it's no good entering one for a show unless you can tie a knot in its neck.

'Though of course the only giraffe I ever knew that was really any use had quite a thick neck. It belonged to a man called Tomkins of Oswaldtwistle, who was so afraid of burglars that he lived in a house with no stairs,

and got up to the first floor and down again by a pet giraffe which would only answer his voice. And in case the burglars put up ladders he taught it to knock ladders down. But it was no good. A burglar made a tape recording of his voice which deceived the giraffe so that it let him climb up it, and he stole Mr Tomkins' evening dress studs and his grandfather clock while he was at the cinema looking at Marlene Dietrich. Believe me, there's nothing to touch magic for dealing with burglars.

I shall laugh if anyone's tried to burgle my flat today. But *he* won't.

'Mr Chandrajotish is over in Dzungaria, but he'll be back in three quarters of an hour for his dinner and our lunch. Let's go and look at the town. O Abdu'l Makkar, thou hast my leave to depart to thy native home in Ruba 'al Khali for the space of two hours, to visit thine aged aunt, on whom be peace. But be not amiss in returning. It is written that the early eagle catcheth the serpent, but the tardy guest findeth the flagon empty. Good afternoon, ladies, don't overfeed Pompey. Aren't Mr Chandrajotish's wives charming?' he added, as he went out into a very narrow lane. 'But he has to spend two or three hours a day on incantations to give them perpetual youth and good temper. He says it's worth it, but it's hard work. Of course Solomon couldn't keep it up, though he was a great magician, but then he had three hundred wives, which I think is too many.'

I'm not going to tell you about Delhi, because you can find out about it in books about India. But I certainly did think the great mosque and the Purana Kila very beautiful, and here is something you won't find in the guide books, though Mr Leakey knew it. You get the world's best sweets very cheap indeed in a little shop on the north side of the Kinara Bazaar. While we were buying them I saw a lovely great pink-eyed mongoose hunting rats in a drain just next door.

We came back to lunch, which was very good. Mr Chandrajotish had come back. He was a jolly, fat man with an immense ruby in his turban, and talked English very well, except that he talked about the railway istation, and said bockus for box. 'I could enchant my-self to ispeak English like a beroadcast announcer,' he said, 'but I think it is more funny to speak like this. When Englishmen first speak Urdu they say "saddle the European" when they want to say "saddle the horse", so why should not I too make mistakes?' We had fish, spiced chicken and rice off gold plates, wine out of cups of solid emerald, and then sweets and mangoes, though they were out of season. But one of Mr Chandrajotish's servants planted a mango stone in the ground under a basket, and lifted the basket four times so that we first saw it growing into a seedling, then into a bush, later flowering, and finally bearing fruit. I didn't think that as good as Mr Leakey's way of getting mangoes, where I saw the tree growing. But I was pleased when the servant threw one end of a rope into the air, climbed up it, and vanished, pulling the rope after him.

'I'm not very good at that,' said Mr Leakey. 'I think you do not pronounce the mantra right,' said Mr Chandrajotish. 'In the word smrita you must bend your tongue back and put it against the roof of your mouth when you pronounce the R. That is where most European sorcerers make a mistake.' Mr Leakey tried it several times, and finally got it right. 'Thank you so much,' he said. 'By the way, I've got some magic books in my hamper that you might like to see.'

We went out into the garden, and for the first time I saw Mr Leakey look really worried. 'Tut tut,' he said, 'this is truly annoying.' The hamper was wide open, and the things out of it lying about. Clementina, who ought to have been tied round it, was on the grass with about

half her body in coils and the other half standing up
and swaying to and fro as if she were drunk. 'Serpents
aren't what they were in my young days,' remarked Mr
Leakey. 'I think my servant Piyari Lal has been charming her,' said Mr Chandrajotish, 'call him here.' We
called, but nobody came. One of the books, written in
some queer writing I didn't know, was open. 'Can he
read Devanagari?' asked Mr Leakey. 'Oh yes, but he is

59

not very good at magic,' said Mr Chandrajotish. 'A good thing too, the book's open at a mantra for turning people into grasshoppers. He might have made us into grasshoppers, and I'm sure I shouldn't be good at chirping. But of course the joke's on him. If he didn't say the spell on page 17 first, he's turned himself into a grasshopper.'

'Well, he is quite a good servant, and we shall have to turn him into a man again. Fortunately I know a spell that will bring all the grasshoppers within a mile here. It is really black magic, the sort of thing that silly young sorcerers use to spoil their neighbours' crops. Fetch my calico drum, darling. That was a great invention of Mr Lear's, one of the best new bits of magic we got from England in the last hundred years. Mr Leakey, will you please wave a circle round my orange trees thrice, I don't want them eaten by grasshoppers. And then protect the grass.'

Mrs Nur-i-dunya Chandrajotish (for that was the name of the jinn wife) came out with an enormous calico drum, and he began dancing round it, quicker than I should have thought so fat a man could. As he went round he beat it with a large purple umbrella, and sang the spell, which Mr Leakey says I may tell you, because it is in a book already anyway, and it doesn't work unless you know the right dance steps.

> 'Calico drum, the grasshoppers come
> The butterfly, beetle, and bee.
> Over the ground
> Around and around
> With a hop and a bound –

> But they never came back
> They never came back
> They never came back
> They never came back to me.'

Meanwhile Nur-i-dunya was flying about over our heads doing something magic. 'To keep out the butterflies, beetles and bees,' said Mr Leakey, in between two circles. There was a tremendous buzzing in the air, and the insects began to arrive. A few butterflies and a huge beetle with a horn like a rhinoceros arrived before the spell to keep them out was finished. After that only grasshoppers came down into the garden. The others stayed flying about over the house. In a minute the air above us was getting dark, and some birds arrived and started catching them. 'We cannot have that,' said Mr Chandrajotish. 'I will not have my guests eaten. Besides, they might eat Piyari Lal. Scare them off please, my love.' Nur-i-dunya flew up through the cloud of insects, and the birds scattered in all directions. When I looked down the whole ground was covered with grasshoppers of all sorts and sizes, from tiny ones like you see in England up to great locusts as big as prawns, and every moment more were coming.

So many butterflies, beetles, and bees were flying over us that it got quite dark, and the servants had to fetch lamps, and also an immense diamond, which shone from inside. By their light we saw a huge crowd of grasshoppers crawling over one another and covering the entire ground and the walls. They made a noise like hundreds of electric bells. We had to shout at the top of our voices to be heard, but Mr Leakey soon shut them up with a spell out of one of the books.

'Can you spot which is Piyari Lal?' he asked.

'No, I cannot. I will try my spell on some of the funnier ones, but it will only work on seven at a time, and there are about a crore, that is to say ten million, here.'

'Don't worry, Abdu'l Makkar ought to be here by now, and he can always pick out an animal that is really an enchanted man or woman. He says they look like Mickey Mouse. Dear dear, he's five minutes late. I shall have to rub my magic ring, after all. I hate to do it, because it gives him a horrid feeling like scraping a knife on a plate, but if he's late that's his look-out. Here goes! These rings are very useful, but it's cruel to rub them whenever you want the jinn, like they used to in Aladdin's time. His lamp belongs to a lady in Vienna now, but her jinn has regular hours of work, and she doesn't have to rub it once a month.'

Abdu'l Makkar suddenly appeared out of the ground, scattering a little cloud of grasshoppers as he came up through them. He looked very unhappy, and started apologizing with all sorts of long words, but Mr Leakey cut him short, and told him to find Piyari Lal. He spotted him almost at once, and caught him quite easily. Then Mr Chandrajotish said a spell over him, and he began to change back into a man. It was most interesting to watch. First he began to swell, and his skin burst, like it always does when a grasshopper moults. The thing that came out was rather like a maggot, and grew very quickly into a pinkish worm; then little knobs came out of the worm at four places, and grew into arms and legs. Then the front part of the worm folded backwards and turned into a head, while fingers and toes sprouted out of the four knobs. All the time it was getting bigger and bigger. In about two minutes there was a man on the grass in front of us, about as frightened as I've ever seen anyone. One thing I thought very odd was that the back of the grasshopper had turned into the front of Mr Piyari Lal. But I told a friend of mine who is a zoologist about it, and he said it was all right, because a grasshopper's heart is at the back, then come his guts, and his nervous system is underneath. So either a grasshopper's back is really his front, or a man's front is really his back.

Piyari Lal turned over on to his front and lay down howling with fright. Mr Chandrajotish said another spell, and he got up, but one side of his face was red and the other green, while his hair was bright purple. 'He will stay like that for a week, and I do not think he will take his evening out tomorrow.' Then we cleared the grasshoppers off a bit of grass round the drum, and Mr Chandrajotish danced round it backwards, saying the 'never came back' part of the spell. All the grasshoppers and the other insects flew away, with a tremendous noise, but it was still dark because the sun had set.

The hamper packed itself again, and Clementina, who was all right by now, tied herself round it. Pompey's brazier was filled up with charcoal, and the carpet spread out. 'I think we might go on round the world,' said Mr Leakey. 'Of course it is night to the east of us, but magic carpets travel much better by night, like radio messages. Where would you like to go in America?' I said I would like to try South or Central America, because I was quite likely to go to North America in an un-magic way, and I had seen a lot of it at the cinema, anyway.

We said good-bye to Mr Chandrajotish and his charming wives, except Nur-i-dunya, who asked if we could give her a lift as far as the islands of Wak-wak, as she wanted to call on a sister who lived there, and fly back by bedtime, but was feeling too lazy to fly both ways. Then we set off south-eastwards. There was a young moon, but from five miles up the stars were so bright that we could see more than I have ever seen before. As we went south all sorts of constellations came up which were new to me. I saw a great river of small stars running down the sky in front of Orion, ending in a very bright one called Achernar, and as Orion and his Big Dog rose in the sky I saw Canopus rising behind the Dog's Tail. In a minute or two we were over the Indian Ocean, which shone like silver in the moonlight. We crossed the Nicobar Islands and the bottom of the Malay Peninsula. I saw the pole star disappear below the horizon. Nur-i-dunya and Abdu'l Makkar were talking like anything in one of the jinn languages. Even Mr Leakey admitted he couldn't follow it very well. But I gathered that Abdu'l Makkar's aunt was troubled because she was growing a lot of extra teeth. And her sight was getting so keen that unless she wore smoked glasses she saw right through things and people, like a surgeon with X-rays, and so she was always running into them. Of course these are some of the things that generally happen to old jinns, just as old people lose their teeth and their eyesight.

After some more sea we saw a great red glow on our right. 'That's one of the volcanoes in Java,' said Mr Leakey, 'we're a little out of our course.' We turned slightly to the left, and in a minute or two were over the Molucca Islands. Of course I knew they were called the islands of Wak-wak, because I had read the story of Hassan of Basra in the Arabian Nights. Nur-i-dunya said good-bye, gave Mr Leakey a kiss, and took a beautiful header off the carpet. 'Now,' said Mr Leakey, 'I think we'll go to Central America. It doesn't matter much which way we go. We're nearly opposite British Guiana on the earth, so it's just 20,000 kilometres anyway.' 'Well, let's go south,' I said, 'over the Pole. It'll be day there.' 'Right you are,' he answered, and south we went. We crossed to Australia nearly by the same route as the air mails go, only about two hundred times as quickly, and went on southwards over the great desert. We saw a lake shining in the moonlight, but no lights of towns. But lots of stars that I did not know rose. First I saw two very odd patches of light like bits of the Milky Way, which Mr Leakey said were called Magellan's clouds. Soon after, as we were flying over the sea south of Australia, we saw the Southern Cross and the Centaur. Later on the sun rose in the south-west, rather to my surprise, though now I think of it it was natural enough. There were clouds below us, but through them I sometimes saw a grey cold-looking sea with icebergs.

'Can we stop when we get to the coast?' I asked. 'I should like to visit some penguins.' 'Certainly,' said

Mr Leakey, 'but we shall want some warm clothes. Even when it's sunny in the Antarctic, it's generally windy. Undo, please, Clementina.' He took out of the hamper two fur coats, some huge boots, thick socks, and other warm clothes which had certainly not been there at Delhi, and a thing like a bit of fire-hose with a woollen lining, into which Clementina crept before she tied herself up again. We came down to a height of only a mile or so, and soon reached a desolate coast with cliffs of ice, and mountains behind. We cruised along for a minute or two till we came to a bay that sloped more gently into the sea. 'This is quite a nice little place,' said Mr Leakey, 'there's a penguin town of about half a million here. About as big as Leeds or Bristol.

'They don't have a bad time. Of course you're going to ask how I know. Well, I do. You probably don't know that I was a penguin myself for about three years. Another magician who was jealous of me turned me into one when I had taken my magic ring off in my bath. And the next thing I knew I was swimming about in the Antarctic Ocean catching pink prawns.* I made quite a good penguin. I thought I should have to spend the rest of my life as one, so I settled down and married. We had two children, but then my poor wife was eaten by a seal, and I found time to make a pentacle of stones, and though of course I couldn't speak a spell, I did a magic dance in it for two days, and became a man again.' 'What happened to the chap who turned you into a penguin?' 'Oh well, I had to deal with him; he's imprisoned inside the statue of the Prince Consort on the Albert

* *Euphausia superba*. They are pink even before they are cooked.

Memorial. He sees quite a lot, but he can't do anything except look solemn. And it's cold at nights. But better than being in a bottle at the bottom of the sea, or head downwards in a well like Harud and Marud.'

We landed on some smooth snow, and had a look at the penguins. Each couple had a round nest of stones, and one of them stayed behind to look after the chick, while the other went to sea to get shrimps. Thousands and thousands were waddling about, looking like rather fat men in evening dress. Others were standing on the edge of the sea on a low cliff of ice which they used as a diving board, and were ragging about, trying to push one another off. But you've probably seen all that in a film, and the Antarctic continent when we went on over it looked very like Admiral Byrd's film of it. It was just a jumble of huge mountains and glaciers with no sign of life. We went on over the south pole, and then northwards above Graham Land till we came to the sea again. We passed over a few ships on their way round Cape Horn, and went on over Tierra del Fuego and South America. It was nice to see grass again. Over Argentina we came down low enough to see some of the great herds of cattle that are put into tins there, and then on we went across Brazil. It was getting fairly hot, so I got a sun helmet and a silk shirt and shorts out of the hamper, and put them on. When I looked down again I could see nothing but a solid green sheet, and it was only when Mr Leakey told me that I realized that it was not grass, but the tops of trees. We came down for a minute over the Amazon river, which was nearly as broad as the English Channel, and yet flowing quite quickly, carrying down huge trees. After some more mountains we came to the sea again at about half-past three by my watch.

'Let's go and look at a volcano,' said Mr Leakey. 'It's quite safe if you put on this amulet, but mind you keep it on when you take off the parachute and lifebelt.' We stopped over an island, which I think was Martinique, where there was a volcano blowing out great clouds of smoke, and making a tremendous noise. I put on the amulet and a pair of asbestos overshoes out of the hamper, and we came down on a black rock just by the edge of the crater, and looked over the cliff into it. I didn't like it a bit. Great blasts of steam and red-hot rocks as big as houses came shooting up past us. I knew I was all right with my amulet, but I couldn't help ducking my head and trying to dodge the rocks. After a minute or two I had had enough of it, and walked down the outside slope of the volcano to see a lava stream that was coming out lower down. It was an ugly, desolate sort of place, more like a slagheap than an ordinary mountain. The ground was all crumbling, and there were no plants. But Pompey thought it was lovely. He jumped off his fire, and flew down after me. I thought he was going to run into me, and I didn't know if my amulet worked against red-hot dragons, even though they were only a foot long. So I jumped to dodge him, and twisted my ankle, because I was on a slope of ashes. Pompey went on down the hill, and started grubbing about in a place where hot steam was coming out. I called up to Mr Leakey, who ran down and had my ankle right in a twinkling with quite a short spell. 'I'm sorry,' he said,

'but I was collecting sulphur. Of course, for magic, one wants sulphur from a volcano, not a chemical factory. And a lot of the volcanoes here are no good. When the Spaniards came over they christened a lot of the volcanoes, because they hoped it would make them better behaved. It didn't stop them erupting, but it did make them quite useless for magic. But no Spaniard ever got near enough to christen this one, because it's rather a fierce volcano. Come back, Pompey, you naughty dragon!' Pompey was paddling about in a lava stream that flowed out just below us, and scratching the slag off the top to get at the red-hot liquid underneath. He drank some, and splashed a great deal more about. I think he heard Mr Leakey all right, though perhaps he didn't, because there was a fearful noise going on. But he

certainly paid no attention. First he rolled over on his back and started kicking his legs in the air. When he got up again his wings were all sticky with lava, like a wasp's when she has been in the treacle. But he scuttled off over the ashes, and took a header into a hole with steam blowing out of it.

Mr Leakey had only to give his ring the tiniest flick to bring Abdu'l Makkar down to us. 'O Abdu'l Makkar,' he said, 'at thy request hath this inmate of the flames and breather of fire accompanied us. It is written that the giver of good advice shall be crowned with garlands, but the evil counsellor shall be cast into a dungeon. Far be it from me to inflict so unfortunate a doom upon thee, but thou must plunge straightway into yonder fiery abyss and retrieve my erring servant. Bind him in chains of brass, or better of tungsten, which hath a higher melting point, and bring him to me. But chastise him not, for he hath been valiant in battle. We precede thee to the isle of Andros.'

Abdu'l Makkar bowed deeply, and went down the hole after Pompey. We climbed up the slope again, and went off on the carpet westwards over the sea to Andros, where we landed on a sandy beach behind a coral reef, and swam out to it. It was about two hundred yards out, and the sea inside it was beautifully calm and warm, though there were big waves outside. The pools on the reef were full of lovely green fish like little parrots, and bright red starfish and sea urchins. I spent a happy half hour there, thanks to a pot of magic ointment which protected me from the sun. When we swam back again Abdu'l Makkar was there with Pompey, who was now chained to the brazier, and looked very sorry for himself. We had tea on the beach, and then went home to England on the carpet. The sun set as we were over the Bay of Biscay. I put on my warm clothes again, and a moment later we were dropping through the clouds towards London.

We came into Mr Leakey's room through the wall, without leaving a hole in it, which felt horrid, because, though I knew nothing would happen, I must admit I don't like running into a brick wall at about ninety miles an hour. So if ever you are taken for a journey on a magic carpet I strongly advise you to shut your eyes at the beginning and end. The room was undisturbed, but there was a shuffling noise from outside. We opened the door, and a most miserable-looking man came into the room. His nose was pulled out into a great pink cord about three feet long, and the end of it was stuck to the door handle. He tried to edge back when he saw Abdu'l Makkar, and the nose stretched out like a piece of rubber. But he couldn't get very far, because the nose was elastic.

'Shall I flay this thief alive, O wisest of the wizards, or shall I disembowel him and fry his liver before his eyes?' asked the jinn. 'Such punishments, O Abdu'l Makkar, are fortunately obsolete in London,' replied Mr Leakey. 'I will not dispute their justice, but they are indubitably messy. You may think yourself lucky,' he said to the thief, 'that we weren't away for the week-end, because I'm the only person who can unstick your nose from that handle except with a hatchet. So if I had died you might never have got away, like Theseus and

Pirithous, who sat down in some magic glue three
thousand years ago, and are sitting there still. Well, I'm
going to let you go because I don't like your face. If you
looked prettier I might keep you as an ornament. You
are a mug, aren't you? I'm not going to tell you you're a
bad man, but you must be a fool to go in for a job as
badly paid as burglary. Anyway you aren't going to be a
burglar any more. I'm going to let your nose go, but the
next time you burgle a house, even if it isn't a magic
one like mine, your nose will stick to it, and they'll have
to get it off with an axe. D'you see this fiery dragon?
When I let you go, I'll set him at you unless you run at
once, so you needn't stop to thank me.' Pompey was
straining at his tungsten leash, so when the nose was let
go that burglar got off the mark before it had quite
shortened to its usual length, and was off down the stairs
so quickly that I thought he would break his neck.

'I'm almost sorry I let him go,' said Mr Leakey, 'he's
got the makings of a hundred yards champion. If I'd
only thought of it I might have made him practise with
Pompey after him. And now, if you'll excuse me, I've got
to conjure up a devil before dinner, because tomorrow
I've got to deal with a sasabonsum who's being a
nuisance in Ashanti, and I may want some help. Oh,
don't you know what a sasabonsum is? I wish people
learned unnatural history like they used to. A sasabonsum is a nasty sort of demon who hangs on to branches
over forest paths by his hands, and catches Negroes
round the neck with his toes. He can use his big toe for
a thumb, like a monkey. Of course he doesn't hurt white
men, because they don't believe in him. But Negroes do,

and that's that. My devil friend's quite a decent devil, as they go, but you might find him rather alarming. So if you don't mind I'll say good-night. Thanks so much for your help with that jinn. Can I take you anywhere by carpet?'

'No, thank you very much,' I said. 'After today I shall feel it quite an adventure to go by bus. I've had a wonderful time and feel as if I'd had a month's holiday. I shall be able to go back to work again on Monday as fit as a fiddle.'

So on Monday I started doing sums about how to make new kinds of primroses and cats; for that is one of my jobs, and I think it is nearly as odd as Mr Leakey's.

Mr Leakey's Party

After our trip round the world I didn't see Mr Leakey again for three months. He hasn't got a telephone, of course, so I couldn't ring him up. I went round to call twice. Once I found his door with a plate on it saying:

'NOAH GOTOBED
Artificial Toenail Manufacturer.
Wholesale Orders only.'

I guessed that was only a joke to keep people away, because a person might want to buy five or ten artificial toenails if their real ones had all been squashed by people treading on them in the tube, but nobody would want to buy a hundred sets. Besides there was a notice posted on the door saying 'Away till Wednesday week,' and no letter box. The next time I went there was just a brick wall where the door ought to have been. After that I gave up going.

About the end of March I was sitting in my bath before going to bed one evening, and had the hot water turned on, as I generally do, because like that it isn't too hot to get into, and stays hot a long time. But I was surprised when a goldfish came out of the tap, because ordinary goldfish die in water that just seems nicely warm to a man. I was still more surprised when I saw he was wearing a panama hat, because I couldn't see how it stuck on. But I nearly jumped out of the bath when he put his head out of the water, took off his hat to me, and started talking. He took his hat off with his right fin, holding the edge between two of the spines, and he talked in rather a low squeaky voice.

'Good evening,' he said. 'I've come from Mr Leakey, and I've got a message for you. Can you come to tea with him about four o'clock in the afternoon on Saturday week? He is giving a party, and you can stay as long as you like. It's going to be a fancy dress party, but he'll provide the dress. He hopes you'll be able to come, because it is going to be a very special party.'

'Just wait a minute,' I said, 'while I get my magic diary. But are you quite comfortable? Don't you mind the heat or the soap in the water? Wouldn't you like me to put you in some cool water in this basin?'

'No thank you,' answered the fish, 'I'm quite comfortable here, and I'm accustomed to heat and soap. You see, I'm not an ordinary goldfish. I live in a geyser in New Zealand, where the water is much hotter than your bath, and it's often soapy, because people throw bars of soap in to make it throw up a jet of steam and hot water. So I'm quite all right.'

I looked at my diary and told him to thank Mr Leakey very much, and say I should be delighted to come. He asked me to turn on the hot water again, and when I did, he jumped back into the tap, like a salmon up a waterfall, and disappeared.

On Saturday of the next week I turned up at Mr Leakey's flat about two minutes to four. On the stairs I met a rather badly dressed boy, and we went in together, for this time the door was there all right. Mr Leakey received us; he was dressed like a real magician, in a huge conical hat covered with runes and pentacles, and a long flowing robe. He introduced me to the boy, and told me he was called Mr John Robinson. I liked that. I think it is very rude to introduce a boy as Johnnie Robinson, or Master Robinson. If boys behave sensibly I think you ought to be just as polite to them as if they were grown-up.

'This is Mr Dobbs, the physicist,' he went on, as he introduced me to a short fat man with a red face and no hair on the top of his head but lots on his chin. 'At least he was a physicist, but he's out of work now. He used to make £3,000 a year out of the railways by travelling with excess luggage.'

'I beg your pardon.'

'Excess luggage. Ordinary people have to pay for theirs, but the railway had to pay to carry his, because it weighed less than nothing, like a balloon. Mr Dobbs had some special bags. When he put them on the weighing machine at the station he pressed a button which opened a thing like a sparklet inside, and let out hydrogen into the bag, so that it pulled upwards, like a balloon.'

'But why didn't it fly up into the air?'

'Ah, that's where Mr Dobbs was clever. The gas coming out of the sparklet thing worked an electro-magnet which pulled up the iron floor of the weighing machine. So they had to pile on weights to make the machine register nothing. You see, if your bag weighs a hundredweight more than it ought to you have to pay the railway company, but if it weighs a hundredweight less than nothing, they have to pay you. The Great North of Scotland Railway, which used to go to Aberdeen, wouldn't pay, but he brought a lawsuit against them, and in the end the House of Lords found he was right, and the railway company had to pay him $4/9\frac{1}{2}$, and £95,000 costs for the lawyers. He went on earning money like this for years, until they passed a special Act of Parliament to stop him. So now he's out of work, but he's got a new scheme for making money out of cinemas. I think he ought to have been a magician.

'This is the archangel Raphael. He's here in case any of my guests get frightened at the things we're going to do. But with the archangel here they'll know it's all right. Of course I wouldn't have troubled him to come, but an archangel can be in as many places as he likes at once, so I'm not interfering with his work or his play. Just now he's helping widows and orphans in Baghdad, Topeka, Split, Whifflet, Semipalatinsk, Sotteville, and Moose Jaw, besides keeping wicket against a team of devils on Inaccessible Island, and picking orchids in a forest in Brazil.'

'I'm extremely proud to meet you,' I said. 'Not at all,' replied Raphael. 'Mr Leakey's being too polite; it's always a pleasure to come to his parties. Besides I like to be able to come like a real archangel, instead of putting my wings in my coat-tails, which is a nuisance if one's wings are feathery like mine, instead of leathery like Abdu'l Makkar's here. Not that I'd change with him, of course.'

Several more guests came. There were three other

boys, four girls, a Chinese-looking man in a yellow woollen cloak who came through the roof, a charwoman, a very smartly dressed lady who turned out to be a movie star on holiday, a devil who came up through the floor,

and a sailor in uniform, from H.M.S. *Furious*. The devil was dressed in a grey top hat and frock coat, like a rather smart gentleman going to Ascot. But I could see he was a devil from his horns, which showed when he took his hat off. Devils always have to wear tall hats if they want to hide their horns. And his tail came out through a hole in his check trousers. He and the arch- angel bowed to one another rather stiffly, but they didn't shake hands, and the end of the devil's tail kept twitch- ing like a cat's. I expect he would have liked to do something nasty to the archangel, only he was too polite to do it in front of Mr Leakey. As the people arrived I noticed the room getting gradually bigger. Two of the walls kept moving away, and a rather odd-looking tree in a golden pot grew chairs on the end of its boughs which dropped off when they were ripe. Besides the chair-tree there were a chocolate-tree and a toffee-tree, which pushed out branches with sweets growing on them to anyone who went near.

'Well,' said Mr Leakey, 'I think we're all here. Now will everyone decide what they want to be for the party. You can be anything you like, only it must be a reason- able size. I mean if somebody wants to be Mount Everest they can, only they mustn't be more than six feet high, or they might easily squash the rest of us. And if anyone wants to be a flea, it must be a flea at least as big as a sheep, or else it might get squashed or lost, and it won't be able to jump more than ten feet, or it might hurt itself on the ceiling.'

'Please, Sir, may I be an elephant?' asked John Robinson. 'That's easy,' said Mr Leakey, and with a mere flick of his wand he made him into a small ele- phant about as big as a pony, but of course with thicker legs. He went round the room in high spirits, shaking everybody's hand and picking fruit with his trunk. Then the movie star, in a rather simpering voice, said she would like to be a butterfly. She was wrong, because you've no idea how ugly a butterfly looks when it's as big as an albatross. Her wings were certainly a pretty colour, but they were covered with rather ugly scales. She had huge goggly eyes on each side of her head, and her proboscis looked like one of those tubes with a vacuum in them that go between two carriages of a train. And she had six rather thin hard black legs with hooks on the ends.

One of the little girls, who wore spectacles, looked as if she worked rather hard at her lessons, and she asked to become William Shakespeare. So she did, and talked nothing but blank verse for the rest of the afternoon, except once or twice when she rhymed. Another girl, who was rather fat, became a tortoise, a giant one of course. Mr Dobbs was turned into a regular icosahedron, which is a thing like a crystal all covered with triangles. He rolled about in a rather awkward sort of way. The charwoman became a princess with a rather small golden crown, and an ermine cloak, which she found very hot before she had done. We called her 'Your serene transparency' because it turned out that she was a German princess. There used to be an awful lot of princes and princesses there, and they were called funny names like that. The real German word is 'durchlaucht', but Mr Leakey said it would take him twenty minutes to bewitch us all into pronouncing German properly, so we said it in English.

One of the other boys became a Rolls-Royce, not a full-size one of course. The chocolate-tree grew a little petrol pump on one of its branches, and filled up his tank, and he went rushing about the room; but he had special magic bumpers to prevent him knocking anyone down. A little girl became a fairy, one of that rather soppy kind all dressed in white and covered with stars, with little wings like a bee's. Another boy became a major-general with a feathery hat and a big white moustache, and rows and rows of medals. He wore spurs which caught in the carpet, and said 'By Gad, Sir.'

The Chinese-looking man, who turned out to be a Tibetan lama, said he didn't much care, because nothing was real anyway, which *I* don't believe is true. But Mr Leakey said it was fun to change one's illusions, so he was turned into a yak, because he said he knew some very nice yaks at home. The last little girl was turned into a boy. I thought she was made into a very ordinary sort of boy, but she seemed quite pleased about it. The sailor became a white bull-terrier, but first he had to promise not to bite the rest of us.

I couldn't think what to become, because I thought there were enough animals and people already, and I didn't want to be a machine. So I asked to be turned into a comet. Of course I was only a little comet, about six feet long, in fact I should think the smallest comet on record, because most comets are bigger than the earth, and some of them millions of miles long.

It feels very queer to be a comet. When I became one, the first thing I felt was a sort of buzzing feeling inside, which went on all the time I was a comet. Then I floated up into the air, and found I was flying round and round one of the lamps. Sometimes I went quite close to it, and then a long way off, but I always kept my head facing the lamp. However after a while I found out how to fly where I wanted, and after about ten minutes I was dancing about in the air with the butterfly, though I think she really preferred dancing with the archangel. You see after all an archangel has got hands to hold on to you with, and a comet hasn't. So I could only spin about near the butterfly, instead of being a real partner. I had a few dances with the fairy, too, but she preferred flitting about and standing on one leg on the tops of the trees.

As soon as I learned how to fly where I wanted, I was able to spare the time to look at what the others were doing, especially while Raphael was dancing with the butterfly.

By that time the two other boys had been transformed. One was turned into a lobster, and a very fine one he made, about six feet long not counting his feelers, and his claws made me feel quite thankful I was up in the air. But he didn't hurt anyone with them. Shakespeare and the princess went for rides on him and the tortoise. The other boy said he wanted to be a ghost. I heard Mr Leakey try to persuade him to try something else. 'You see,' he said, 'you'll probably be a ghost anyway for a very long time, whether you want to be or not, whereas if you don't choose to be something else today, you may never get another chance to be a gorgonzola cheese, or a vacuum cleaner, or George Robey,

or an aposiopesis, whatever that may be.' However the boy said he wanted to be a ghost, so Mr Leakey said he would change him into one, only he had to promise not to go near the window, because if anyone passing by in the street saw a ghost at the window they might think someone had been murdered, and send for the police.

I didn't see him turned into a ghost, because at that moment I had got rather entangled in the branches of the toffee-tree. But the moment he did there was rather a squabble. The devil tried to catch him because he said he hadn't done his homework, and Raphael said that didn't count because he was always very nice to his mother, and only last week he had helped a blind man across the street, and rescued a dog that had fallen into a coal-hole.

However Mr Leakey managed to persuade both of them that it was their afternoon off, and the ghost had great fun. He tried to frighten the bull-terrier, but only made him angry, so that he jumped right through him. Then he tried it on William Shakespeare, who said:

'Thou art too like the Prince of Denmark's father
To fright a poet who hath acted him.'

Next he tried to drive the Rolls, but though he managed to get his head and half his body in through the shut door, it was so small that there was no room for his legs. I think a ghost looks very funny when you can only see the bottom half of it, which by the way happens oftener than you think.

When I was an undergraduate at New College,

Oxford, there used to be a ghost there who had been walking on the second floor ever since King Charles I's time. Well, about fifty years ago they rebuilt part of the college, and made the rooms on the first floor a good deal higher. But the ghost went on walking where the old floor had been, and the people who lived in the first-floor rooms used to see his boots sticking down through the ceiling. They were great long boots too. A man I knew extremely well said you could see the soles of them quite clearly, and one of them wanted mending. Of course I don't know how quick ghostly boots get worn out, but you can't be surprised, for he had been walking in them for nearly three centuries, even if he has had only the ghost of a floor to walk on lately.

Anyway people soon got accustomed to this particular ghost at Mr Leakey's party, and I must say, though of course it was funny to see through him, he didn't look as alarming as a lobster the size of a lion.

Soon after this Mr Leakey said it was time for tea, and he would change the shapes of anyone who thought they couldn't have any. Mr Dobbs and I both asked to be changed, for neither an icosahedron nor a comet has a mouth. The ghost said he would try to eat and drink, but Mr Leakey said no, he didn't think it would be nice to watch tea and chewed-up cake going down into his inside. The lobster wanted to try too. He said he was sure he could hold a cup in his claws. Mr Leakey said that was all right, but he couldn't drink tea with a mouth that opened sideways instead of up and down.

So Mr Dobbs went back to a man, because the next thing he wanted to be hadn't got a mouth either. The ghost, who was a little grumpy, asked to be turned into a fire engine, because he thought like that he would be able to drink tea very quickly. But Mr Leakey turned him into one of the kind that, instead of squirting water, throws froth on to burning oil, so after all he didn't drink so much more tea than the rest of us.

I became a toucan. This was before the Guinness advertisements, so I didn't ask for beer. It is a little difficult to balance one's beak just at first, and even at the end of the party I found that when I lifted my head suddenly I involuntarily stuck my tail out too. But I found flying quite easy. I flew up on to the chocolate-tree and watched the lobster being turned into a flying phalanger like the ones in the house on the north side of the canal at the Zoo, only bigger. Mr Leakey thanked us for giving him such easy jobs. 'You see, turning people into animals is almost natural. Only a few million years ago our ancestors were animals, and I expect our descendants will be animals too, and rather nasty ones, if the human race doesn't learn to behave itself a bit better. Turning people into animals is one of the oldest and simplest sorts of magic. Don't you remember how Circe turned Ulysses' sailors into pigs? And even now a lot of people get turned into pigs every year by eating too much enchanter's nightshade.* There's plenty of it in Wiltshire, which may account for the excellent hams you get from there.

'I knew a boy called Ernest Higginbotham who was very greedy. He was asked to a picnic in a wood near Chilmark in Wiltshire, where the stone for the Houses

* *Circaea lutetiana.*

of Parliament came from. The tea was coming on in a dogcart (that was before the time of motor cars), and the wheel came off, so they didn't get any. He said he was very hungry, and ate about a peck of enchanter's nightshade. So he became a pig—a Gloucester Old Spots, to be accurate.

'Well, his father thought of showing him at circuses as a Learned Pig who could read. But he had an uncle who was a professor of Greek, and this uncle remembered that the proper treatment was a plant called Moly, which Ulysses had used. But he didn't know what it looked like. So next spring he and the professor of Botany went off in a ship to Greece with Ernest the pig and Sibthorpe's *Flora Graeca*, and they went solemnly through that book giving him bits of every plant in it to eat till they found one that changed him back. And then they knew it must be Moly, and wrote a paper about it in one of those odd magazines that professors read.

'But even after he stopped being a pig Ernest kept the spots, and was spotty all his life. And though he was still greedy he would never touch a sausage.

'Well now you're all changed, let's go and have tea.'

The wall at the other end of the room suddenly began to go queer. It had a wallpaper on it with pictures of flowers, which became real flowers and tumbled down on to the floor. We flew, walked, crawled, or drove over them and sat down round a beautiful table with the oddest-looking things on it and round it. There were chairs for some of the guests. I had a lovely perch with jewels on it to match my feathers. The butterfly sat on a huge flower about a yard across, the elephant stood on four little barrels like they do at circuses. The tortoise, who would have been late for tea if she hadn't caught hold of the Rolls and been pulled along, was lifted up to the table on a thing with a flat top rather like a piano stool.

Everyone had a teacup, but there were no pots. However, when we pressed buttons in front of us little fountains of tea and milk squirted out of holes in the table into our cups. I found that I could hold on to the perch with one foot and lift the cup with the other, but my beak wasn't very good for drinking with, so I found it best to open it wide and let the fountains play into it, which they did without spilling a drop.

The fire engine found it easy enough to suck up tea, and started blowing wonderful bubbles, but the Rolls-Royce had more of a job. He didn't want to miss his tea, and came up to the table for it, but nobody knew whether to put it into his petrol tank or his radiator, and Mr Leakey wouldn't tell them because he said he didn't know anything about machinery. William Shakespeare said:

> 'Chameleons feed on air and worms on earth;
> This magic car shall thrive on Indian leaf,'

and suggested the petrol tank. But Mr Dobbs said he thought the tea came from Ceylon and would choke his carburettor, and in spite of what Hamlet said, chameleons really eat flies. So they unscrewed his radiator cap and poured the tea in there. When he had a mouth again to talk with he said it tasted very good.

Besides tea we had all kinds of lovely cakes and sandwiches. I began with caviar, which as you know comes from a sturgeon. It is so good that if anyone catches a sturgeon in England he has to give it to the King. So it is called a Fish Royal, and a lot together are called a Royal College of Sturgeons, or at least that was what Mr Leakey told me. He said this caviar had been swimming about in the Caspian sea that morning and Abdu'l Makkar had got it from a jinn who lived there, and was a communist, and had brought it back on the magic carpet.

I'm not going to tell you about the cakes and ices and fruit, because you might think I was greedy if I said how much I liked them. Of course toucans like much the same things as people do—the ones at the Zoo are very fond of chocolates and grapes. The bull-terrier got a raw beefsteak and a lovely great marrow bone. The Rolls, besides tea, was given some petrol of the very expensive sort that is generally kept for aeroplanes. The elephant ate cakes like the rest of us. So did the yak, rather to my surprise. The tortoise was given a special kind of plant rather like a cabbage, brought all the way from the Galapagos Islands, where that kind of tortoise lives. The butterfly sucked up honey through her proboscis, which was almost as thick as the elephant's trunk. And the devil ate six boxes of matches and a tablespoonful of Cayenne pepper washed down with half a pint of fuming sulphuric acid.*

After tea Mr Dobbs asked to be changed into an atom of caesium, because that is the fattest kind of

* $H_2S_2O_7$.

atom, though of course much too small to see. But this was a specially big one, about four feet across. He was quite round, and full of bits buzzing round the middle. They were buzzing so quick that one could never see them properly. There was one bit that sometimes came right out and once or twice shot across the room. Mr Dobbs said that happens when atoms get excited. However, he always got that bit back again, and gave a lovely flash of light when he did. We started playing musical chairs. The yak, the tortoise, the elephant, the car, and the fire engine were chairs, and Mr Leakey made five other chairs by just sitting down. He seemed to sit down on nothing, and looked as if he would get a nasty bump, but when he got up there was a chair there.

He stayed sitting down on the last of the chairs and played a tune on a piano that wasn't there. It was a funny game, because five of the chairs were playing themselves and kept moving about. Most of the people stayed near the magic chairs, and tried to get into them, but when the tune stopped one of them vanished, and the princess and the bull-terrier, who were both waiting to sit on it, made a sudden rush for the yak. The dog jumped on to him, but fell over on the other side. However, he got on to the car, and Mr Dobbs, the caesium atom, got left out. The next round Mr Shakespeare was left standing, and the round after that the Major-General, who was rather fat. Then there was a great squabble because the little girl who had been turned into a boy said it wasn't fair that the fairy, the butterfly, the toucan, and the archangel should be allowed to fly. So we agreed to keep on the ground, provided we could use our wings to help us to hop. But the next round I was out because my tail got caught in the fairy's skirts, which were very frilly. So it went on until only the devil, the dog, and the boy were left competing for the elephant and the fire-engine.

Then suddenly the door opened, and Pompey the dragon came dashing in, breathing flames and squeaking with pleasure. Of course he was only a very little dragon, but I didn't want my feathers burned, so I flew up into the air. Most of the others ran away too, except the devil, who I suppose was quite accustomed to that sort of thing, and the fire-engine, who squirted a great mass of bubbles at him. Pompey sneezed like anything, and sparks flew all over the room. One of them set the fairy's dress alight, but the engine put her out before she was hurt. Abdu'l Makkar made a dive at Pompey, but he dashed under the elephant's legs, and I don't know what wouldn't have happened if Mr Leakey hadn't turned himself into a pair of tongs, thrown himself along the floor, and grabbed Pompey by the tail. I couldn't help thinking he ought to have been a rugger player, for it was a wonderful tackle.

They soon had Pompey chained up, and looking very much ashamed of himself. Mr Leakey was quite grumpy. 'O abominable among the Ifreets,' he said to Abdu'l Makkar, almost before he had stopped being tongs and was a man again, 'did I not command thee that this breather of flames should be confined in the furnace beneath the kitchen boiler, that he might heat the water for my bath?'

'Thou didst so command, O sovereign of sorcerers,

and it was done according to thy behest. I know not what fell enchanter hath released him from his durance.'

However, he soon found out, for next moment a plumber came into the room. I could tell he was a plumber because of the thing like a giant spanner he carried. ''Ere, wot d'yer teik me for?' he said. 'I'm not St George. I come to mend the water pipes, not to kill no blinking dragons.' Then he suddenly saw the party and opened his eyes and mouth very wide indeed.

'Sit down,' said Mr Leakey, 'and have some tea with us. I know you're not St George, and I'm sure you don't want to kill my dragon. In any case St Saturninus, who is an expert on lead, is the patron of plumbers.' Meanwhile he was pointing his wand at the plumber, who gradually stopped goggling and began to grin. 'I've 'ad me tea, thank you, Sir,' he said.

'Nevertheless, O Abdu'l Makkar, his occupation engendereth thirst. And it is written that King Solomon, upon whom be peace, stayed his guests with flagons. Bring therefore a flagon of bitter, and stay the protector of pipes therewith.'

The plumber drank the flagon and went back to his work. I think in spite of all Mr Leakey's magic, he thought the party a bit queer, and wasn't really sorry to leave. Some people are like that.

After that we played tig and several other games, but I won't tell you about them, because I expect you have heard enough by now. I lost one of my tail feathers when the devil caught me, and the tortoise had to be speeded up with a special charm. I've never seen a tortoise running before or since. But this one was quite good at it, and skidded round corners like a racing motorist.

Then the devil said he really had to get away to tempt a Scottish presbyterian minister to go to a dance. He said it was an awfully hard job, and he didn't care to take it on, but of course he had to obey orders. And some of the others said they would have to be going too.

'Well, this is very sad,' said Mr Leakey, 'but I do hope you've enjoyed yourselves. I suppose you all want to be changed back. Toucans and tortoises get shut up in cages in London, and fire-engines are made to work quite hard. But I could change any of your names if you like.'

'What's in a name?' said Shakespeare. 'The rose by any other name would smell as sweet.' 'Oh no it wouldn't,' said Mr Leakey. 'Not if it were called the Lesser Stinkwort, or the Fish-and-chips-flower. Names matter more than you think. I knew a man called Phipps who was an ironmonger, somewhere in north London. He was quite happy in his shop, and after dinner he liked to take his boots off in the parlour and play patience. But his wife wouldn't let him. She said he must go out of the room to take his boots off, and that patience was a silly game, which it is, but no sillier than a lot of others. So he said, "Let's get divorced." But she wouldn't have that either.

'So Mr Phipps thought of a plan. First he became enormously rich, by selling more rabbit wire and claw-hammers than anyone else in London. Then he bought a house at Ugley, which is rather a nice place on the road from Epping to Cambridge. Then he gave so much money to hospitals and churches and schools and liberals and welfare workers and so on that they decided to make him a lord. So when they asked him what he would be called he said Lord Ugley. The king laughed like anything, but Mr Phipps had his way.

'So then his wife was called Lady Ugley, and she didn't like it a bit. So she got divorced and married a man called Lovely, and I suppose she lived happily ever after. Then Lord Ugley gave away the rest of his money, and only kept his shop. And he takes off his boots and plays patience every evening. But if he'd become Lord Golders Green or Lord Moreton-in-the-Marsh or something like that it would have been quite different.'

Mr Leakey was only asked to change two names. A girl called Victoria became Irene, which means Peace, and a boy called Augustus became Tom.

Then we all stood in a row, and Mr Leakey got Abdu'l Makkar to take a photograph of us, but it isn't very good because the butterfly waggled her wings in the middle, and the boy started laughing at Pompey, who was trying to drink petrol from the pump, and had set it alight.

When the photograph was taken we all shut our eyes, or switched off our lamps, except the atom, who was told to look like xenon, whatever that means. I don't know what Mr Leakey did while our eyes were shut, but when we opened them again we were just ordinary people. Some of us went home by magic carpet, some by tube, and some by bus. I walked back, and when I got home I found a present waiting for me, a beautiful book about comets, and another about birds with coloured pictures of four different sorts of toucan, one of which was the sort that I had been.

I haven't seen Mr Leakey since then. If I ever do I will let you know. But I think I saw Raphael last week. He was dressed as an ordinary sort of workman, and was helping an old lady who had fallen down in the street and sprained her ankle. So perhaps I shall see Mr Leakey again too.

Rats

Once upon a time there was a man called Smith. He was a greengrocer and lived in Clapham. He had four sons. The eldest was called George, after the king, and it was arranged that he was to inherit his father's shop. So at school he went to special botany classes, and learned about the hundred and fifty-seven different kinds of cabbage, and the forty-four sorts of lettuce. And he went to zoology classes and learned about the seventy-seven kinds of caterpillar that live in cabbages, and how the green kind come out if you sprinkle the

cabbages with soapy water, and the striped ones with tobacco juice, and the big fat brown ones with salt water. So when he grew up he was the best greengrocer in London, and no one ever found caterpillars in his cabbages.

But Mr Smith only had one shop, so his other three

sons had to seek their own fortunes. The second son was called Jim, but his real name was James, of course. He went to school and he won all the prizes for English essays. He was captain of the school soccer team, and played half-back. And he was very clever at all sorts of tricks, and used to play them on the masters. One day he stuck a match-head into the chalk. It wasn't a safety-match head either, but one of those blue and white ones that strike on anything. So when the master started writing on the board he struck the match and nobody did much work for the next five minutes. Another day he put methylated spirits in the ink-pots, and the ink wouldn't stick to the pens. It took the master half-an-hour to change all the ink, so they didn't get much French done that hour, and he hated French, anyway. But he never did ordinary tricks like putting putty in the key-holes or dead rats in the master's desk.

The third son was called Charles, and he was fairly good at mathematics and history, and got into the cricket eleven as a slow left-handed bowler, but the only thing he was really good at was chemistry. He was the only boy in his school (or in any other, for all I know) who had ever made paradimethylaminobenzaldehyde or even arabitol (which is really quite hard to make, and has nothing to do with rabbits). He could have made the most awful smells if he had wanted to, because he knew how. But he was a good boy and didn't. Besides if he had they might have stopped him doing chemistry, and he wanted to go on doing chemistry all his life.

The fourth son was called Jack. He wasn't much good at any of his lessons, nor at games either. He never managed to kick a ball straight, and he went to sleep when fielding at cricket. The only thing he was any good at was wireless. He made pretty well everything in the

set at home, except the valves, and he was learning to make them when the story begins. He had a great-aunt Matilda who was so old that she said she could remember the railway from London to Dover being built. She couldn't walk, and had to stay in bed all the time. He made her ear-phones to listen in with, and she said she hadn't been so happy since Queen Victoria's time. Jack was very clever with other electrical things too. He made a special dodge to get electric light for his father's house without paying for it, and the meter didn't register anything for a week. Then his father found out what was happening and said, 'We mustn't do that, it's stealing from the electric light company.' 'I don't think it's stealing,' said Jack. 'A company isn't a person, and besides the electricity goes through our lamps and back again to the main. So we don't keep it, we only borrow it.' But his father made him take his gadget down, and even paid the company for the current, for he was an honest man.

Mr Smith had a daughter named Lucille, but everyone called her Pudgy. She doesn't really come into the story, so I shan't say anything more about her till the end, except that when she was little her front teeth stuck out; but in the end they managed to push them in.

Now at this time there was a great plague of rats in the London Docks. They were specially fierce rats, whose ancestors had come on steamers from Hong Kong along with tea and ginger and silk and rice. These rats ate all sorts of food which are brought to London in ships because we cannot grow enough food in England to feed all the people here. They ate wheat from Canada and cheese from Holland, and mutton from New Zealand and beef from Argentina. They bit out pieces from the middle of Persian carpets to line their nests, and wiped their feet on silk coats from China.

Now the man who is at the head of all the docks in London is called the Chairman of the Port of London Authority, and he is a very big bug indeed. He has an office near Tower Hill that is almost as big as Buckingham Palace. He was awfully angry about the rats, because he has to look after the cargoes that are brought in ships from the time they are unloaded till they are taken away in trains and lorries and carts. So he had to pay for the things the rats ate. He sent for the best rat-catchers in London. But they only caught a few hundred rats, because they were a very cunning kind of rat. They had a king who lived in a very deep hole, and the other rats brought him specially good food. They brought him chocolate that had come from Switzerland, bits of turkey from France, dates from Algiers, and so on. And he told the other rats what to do. If any rat got caught in a trap, he sent out special messengers to give warning of the danger. He had an army of ten thousand of the

bravest young rats, and they used to fight any other animals that were sent against them. A terrier can easily kill one or two rats; but if a hundred rush at him all at once, he may kill three or four of them, but the others will kill him in the end. The rats with the toughest teeth were trained to be engineers, and used to bite through the wire of rat-traps to let prisoners out.

So in one month these rats killed a hundred and eighty-one cats, forty-nine dogs, and ninety-five ferrets. And they wounded a lot of others so badly that they ran away if they even smelt a rat, let alone saw one. And they let out seven hundred and forty-two prisoners from six hundred and eighteen traps. So the rat-catchers lost their best dogs and ferrets and traps, and gave up the job in despair. The people in the docks sent round to

the chemists' shop for all sorts of rat poison, and sprinkled it about mixed with different sorts of bait. But the king rat gave orders that none of his subjects were to eat food unless it came straight out of a box or a barrel or a bag. So only a few disobedient rats got poisoned, and the others said it served them right. And the poison was no more use than the dogs and ferrets and traps.

So the Chairman of the Port of London Authority called a meeting of the Authority in the great Board Room of his office, and said, 'Can you suggest what is to be done about the rats?' So the Vice-Chairman suggested putting an advertisement in the papers. The next week advertisements came out in all the papers. It took up a whole page, and was printed in huge letters, so that almost everyone in England read it. All the Smith family read it except great-aunt Matilda, who never read the papers, because she listened in to all the broadcast news.

Now this advertisement made all the competitions in the papers look pretty silly. For the Chairman of the Port of London Authority offered a hundred thousand pounds and his only daughter in marriage to the man who would rid the docks of rats. (If the winner was married already, of course, he wouldn't be allowed to marry the daughter, but he got a diamond bracelet for his wife as a consolation prize.) There was a photograph of the hundred thousand pounds; and they were real golden sovereigns, not paper notes. And there was a photograph of the daughter, who was very pretty, with short curly golden hair and blue eyes. Besides this, she could play the violin, and had won prizes for cookery, swimming, and figure skating. The only snag was that the competitors had to bring their own things for killing the rats, so really it cost a lot of money to go in for the competition.

Still thousands and thousands of people went in for it. They had to get three extra postmen to take the letters to the Chairman the next morning. And so many people rang him up on the telephone that the wires melted. For months and months all sorts of people tried their luck. There were chemists and magicians, and bacteriologists and sorcerers, and zoologists and spiritualists and lion hunters, but none of them were able to kill more than a few rats. What was worse, they interfered with the unloading of the ships, and quite a lot of corn had to be sent round by Liverpool and Cardiff and Hull and Southampton instead of London.

Among the people who tried their luck were Jim and Charles and Jack Smith. Jim thought that if only he could make a trap that looked quite ordinary, he would be able to fool the rats, just as he used to fool the masters at school. Now he knew that there were all sorts of old tins lying about the docks, so he designed a special sort of trap made from an old tin. The rats smelt the bait inside it and jumped on to the top. But the top was a trap-door, and so the rat fell through and couldn't get out again. He spent all his spare time making these traps, and he got his friend to help. He borrowed ten pounds from his father, and got Bill Johnson, who was an out-of-work tinsmith, to make more for him. In the end he had one thousand three hundred and ninety-four of these traps; but seventeen of them were pretty bad, so he didn't bring them.

He went along to Tower Hill with his traps on one of his father's carts, and saw the Vice-Chairman, who was a duke, and was looking after all the rat-catching. The Vice-Chairman said, 'Of course these traps aren't enough to go all around all the docks, but we will try them on one.' So they tried them on the West India Dock, where the ships come from Jamaica and the other islands round it, with sugar and rum and treacle and bananas. I don't think that was a very good place to choose, because the rats there are quite specially quick and nimble. This is because they are constantly tumbling into barrels and vats and hogsheads and demijohns of treacle. The slow ones get stuck in it, and that is the end of them. Only the quick ones escape. So all the rats round there are very quick, and good climbers.

Half Jim's traps were baited with cheese and half with bacon. The first night they caught nine hundred and eighteen rats. Jim was terribly pleased, and thought he was going to win the prize. But the next night they only caught three rats, and the third only two. The king rat had warned all his subjects to avoid tins, and only stupid or disobedient ones got caught. On the fourth night they moved the traps to the Victoria Docks, but they only caught four rats. The warning had been spread. So Jim went home very sad. He had wasted a lot of time and ten pounds, and the other boys at school called him Tinned Rats.

Charles Smith had quite a different scheme. He invented a special kind of poison with no taste or smell. I am not going to tell you what it was, or how to make it, because some murderer might read this story, and use it to kill all sorts of people. He made a lot of this poison, and he also made a lot of the stuff that gives the smell to Roquefort cheese, which is a very cheesy kind of cheese made in France. This is called methyl-heptadecyl ketone, and I think it has a lovely smell. Some other people don't like it, but rats do. He borrowed twenty pounds from his father, and got a hundred cheap and nasty cheeses. Then he cut each into a hundred bits. He soaked them first in the poison, and then in the stuff with the Roquefort smell, and put them into ten thousand cardboard boxes. He thought that if he did that the rats would not think that they were ordinary poisoned bait, which is just scattered about, and not in boxes at all. But the boxes were cardboard, so that the rats could get in quite easily.

All through one day two men with wheelbarrows went round the docks, leaving the ten thousand cheese boxes

in different places. And Charles went behind them with a squirt, and squirted the cheesy stuff over them. The whole of East London smelt of cheese that afternoon. When the sun set, the rats came out, and they said to one another, 'This must be a marvellous cheese, quite a little box of it smells as much as a whole case of ordinary cheeses.' So a great many of them ate it. They even brought some back to the king rat. But luckily for him he had just had a huge meal of walnuts and smoked salmon and wasn't hungry. The poison took some time to work, and it wasn't until three o'clock in the morning that the rats began to die of it. The king at once suspected the cheese, and sent out messengers to warn his subjects against it.

Also there was a wicked rat which had been sentenced to death for eating its own children, and the king made it eat the bit of cheese that had been brought him. When it died he knew the cheese was poisoned, and sent out another lot of messengers. The next morning they picked up four thousand five hundred and fourteen dead rats, and ever so many more were dead in their holes, besides others that were ill. The Chairman was so pleased that he gave Charles the money to buy another lot of cheeses. But when, two days later, they left them about, only two out of eight thousand boxes had been opened. So they knew the rats had been too clever for them again. Charles was very sad indeed. He had been so sure of success that he had ordered a wedding ring for his marriage with the Chairman's daughter, and written to the Archbishop of Canterbury to marry them. Now he had to write to the jeweller and the Archbishop to say he wasn't going to marry after all. And worst of all, the cheesy smell stuck to him for a month. They wouldn't have him back at school, and he had to sleep in the coal shed at home.

Last of all Jack tried his plan. It needed a lot of money, and though he borrowed thirty pounds from his father, it was not enough. But he borrowed some more from me, and sold some wireless sets that he had made, until he gradually got all he needed. He bought some very fine iron filings, much finer than the ordinary kind, and had them baked into biscuits. The biscuits were left about the docks. At first the rats would not touch them, but later they found they did them no harm, and began to eat them. Meanwhile Jack got seven perfectly enormous electro-magnets, which were put in different docks. Each was in the middle of a deep pit with smooth sides. And cables were laid so that current from the District Railway and the East London Railway could be put through the magnets. Luckily Jack knew the head electrical engineer on the underground railways, because they were both keen on wireless, so he was able to arrange to borrow their current. When he thought that the rats had eaten enough iron filings he made arrangements to turn the current through the magnets. All loose iron, steel, or nickel things had to be tied up. And the ships, because they are made of steel and iron, had to be tied up very tight indeed with extra cables. And all the people in the docks that night had to wear special boots or shoes with no nails in them; except the Vice-Chairman who was a duke, so of course he had gold nails in his boots.

At half-past one in the morning the last underground railway train had stopped, and they turned all the current that had been working the trains into the first magnet. A few rusty nails and tin cans came rushing towards it, and so did the rats, but more slowly. They were full of iron filings, and the magnet just pulled them. Soon the hole round that magnet was full of rats, and they switched the current on to the next magnet. Then they turned on the third magnet, and so on. Of course only the rats that were above ground were pulled into the holes by the magnets. But they turned them on again and again, and as more and more came out of their holes they were caught too.

The king rat knew something was going wrong, and felt himself pulled to one side of his hole. He sent out messengers, but they never came back. At last he went out himself, and a magnet pulled him into one of the pits. When morning came they turned on water taps and drowned all the rats that had been caught by the magnets. These rats weighed a hundred and fifty tons. No one ever counted them, but they reckoned to have caught three-quarters of a million.

There were some awkward accidents. A night-watchman called Alf Timmins had forgotten to wear boots without nails. So the magnet pulled him along feet first. He managed to get his boots off just as he was on the edge of the rat pit, but a rat hung on to each of his toes, and the magnet pulled these rats so hard that all his toes came off. So now he has no toes, like the Pobble, and takes a smaller size in boots than he used to. But another watchman called Bert Higgs had better luck. Before the war he had been a great billiard-player, but he got a bit of a shell into his brain, and couldn't play billiards any more. And none of the doctors could get the bit out. So when Jack turned the magnet on the bit of shell came popping out of his head, and the part of his brain that made him so good at billiards started working again. So now he is billiard-champion of Poplar.

The next night they turned on the magnets again, and caught a lot more rats, about a hundred tons. Their king

was dead, so they did not know what to do. The third
night they caught a lot more again. After that the few
rats that were left were so frightened that they all ran
away. Some got on to ships and went abroad. Some went
into London, and were a great nuisance to the people
there, but none stayed in the docks. They caught none
the fourth night, and though they hunted with dogs and
ferrets the next day, there wasn't a rat in the place.

So Jack Smith got the hundred thousand pounds and

married the Chairman's daughter on a ship at sea. He didn't want to be married in church, and he thought registrars' offices were ugly, so he hired a ship, and when they were three miles from shore the captain married them, which he couldn't have done if they had been only two and a half miles away, because that is the law. They had two boys and two girls, and Jack got a very good job with the B.B.C. as an engineer. With all that money he might have lived all his life without doing any work, but he was so fond of wireless that he wanted to go on working at it.

His sister married the duke, so she is a duchess; but of course duchesses aren't so important now as they used to be. She has diamond heels to her shoes to match her husband's gold nails. He gave his brothers Jim and Charles money to start in their professions. So Jim spent it on magic wands and trick hats and tables, and became a conjuror, and a very good one too. And Charles went to the University and became a professor of chemistry. I am a professor too, and I know him quite well. So they all lived happily ever after.

The Snake with the
Golden Teeth

There was once a man called Paolo Maria Encarnaçao Esplendido. He lived at Manaos in Brazil. He was a very rich man. He owned two gold mines and a silver mine.

You might think one got more money from a gold mine than a silver mine because gold is worth more than silver. But, as a matter of fact, more money goes down gold mines than comes out of them, because people are always digging mines for gold in places where there isn't enough to make it worth their while.

Senhor Esplendido's gold mines weren't of that sort. He got a fair amount of money out of them, but a lot more from the silver mine. One reason why he was so rich was that he paid the miners very badly. So people didn't like him very much.

Now when people have a lot of money some of them spend it on things like hospitals and universities and parks and picture-galleries, so they are some use. Others buy diamonds and racehorses, so they aren't any use to anyone. Senhor Esplendido was one of the useless kind. But because he lived where he did, he spent it mostly on different sorts of things from what rich men in England buy. The roads round there are so bad that it is no fun motoring. So he only had one car.

But he had three motor-boats, because in that part of Brazil people use the rivers instead of roads. Of course, Manaos is at the place where the Amazon river joins the Rio Negro, so he had lots of water for boating. These motor-boats had all their fittings made of silver, for swank. He gave his wife some diamond bracelets for swank, too, and they had to be very big ones, because she was so fat. And inside his house he had all sorts of golden things made of the gold from his gold mines. All his tooth-brushes had gold handles; he had golden forks and spoons and ash-trays and soap-dishes and door-handles, and he wore a different gold watch every day of the week.

He had a lot of animals that he kept in a private menagerie. I think his liking for animals was the only nice thing about him. For a person who is fond of animals can't be nasty all through. He had some of all the sorts of animals bigger than a mouse that live in Brazil.

He had seven caimans, which are the sort of crocodiles that live there. They look fairly like the crocodiles from India, but they have two holes in their upper jaw to fit the two biggest teeth in their under jaw, which most of the Indian ones haven't. Also they are different from the alligators which live in the United States of America. Some of them are twenty feet long.

He had three jaguars, and two anacondas, which are large snakes that live in Brazil, nearly as big as pythons. They are not poisonous, but they can squash people by twisting round them. They are very good at swimming.

One of them was a she-snake, and he used to have her eggs boiled, and eat them in a golden egg-cup with a golden spoon. He said they were very good, but he was such an awful swanker that very likely they weren't good at all. I don't know, because I have never eaten one. The only man I know who has is an explorer called Mr McOstrich. He ate three at a sitting, but then he hadn't had any food for a week before, so no wonder he liked them.

Now caimans, and for that matter all sorts of crocodiles, are stupid beasts; they can't generally learn anything. Though their heads are so big their brains are smaller than a rabbit's, let alone a dog's or a monkey's or a man's. So they are only wound up to do quite a few sorts of things. A dog has a bigger brain, so he can do thousands of different sorts of things. A man has a bigger brain still, so he can do millions.

But one of these crocodiles must have had a bigger brain than usual, because it learned to do one or two tricks. It was taught by a man called Pedro Rodriguez, whose job it was to look after the beasts. He was very fond of animals and very patient too. He taught this crocodile to come out of the water when he called it. Its name was Rosa.

I forgot to say it was a she-crocodile. Perhaps I ought to say a hen-crocodile, as one says a hen-lobster. For, after all, crocodiles are rather like lobsters in some ways. They live in the water, and are hard outside and can nip you. But crocodiles are not as good to eat as lobsters. Or perhaps I ought to say Rosa was a cow-crocodile. Anyway, it doesn't much matter, because next time I talk about her I will just call her Rosa.

Well, Rosa learned to do several other things. She could sit up on her tail and two hind legs, and open

her mouth for people to throw her food. And she could put her tail in her mouth and waddle round after it. Her husband, who was called Joao, which is Portuguese for John, was stupid and grumpy. At least he was grumpy to men, and would have been to Rosa, only she kept him in order, and used to smack him with her tail if he was greedy, and didn't let her have a fair share of his food.

Well, one day Senhor Esplendido asked Pedro Rodriguez how the animals were. And he said, 'They are all very well, sir, except the he-anaconda, who has broken two of his teeth, but I expect he will grow some more.'

'Nonsense,' said Senhor Esplendido. 'He is grown-up, and can't grow any more teeth.'

Pedro just said, 'Very good, sir,' because he knew it was no use answering back, even if he was right. His master was a very conceited man, and got very angry if you found him out in a mistake.

And then Senhor Esplendido had a great idea. He thought he would have the snake's teeth stopped with gold, so that he would be the only person in the world to have a snake with golden teeth. Because all sorts of people have gold spoons and watches and salt-cellars, and things like that. And some of the kings and princes in India have the oddest things made from gold. The Akoond of Swat had seven wives with gold nose-rings. The Jam of Las Bela has seventeen golden toothpicks, five golden parrot cages, and a golden foot-scraper. The Begum of Bhopal had a golden sewing machine. She was an old lady, and quite intelligent, but she always went about with her head in a bag because she thought it would never do if people saw her face. And the Nono of Spiti has a golden spittoon. (You may think I have made up the Nono of Spiti. But I haven't. There really is a place called Spiti in the Himalaya mountains in latitude thirty-two north and longitude seventy-eight east, and the king of it is called the Nono. I can't help it if people and places have funny names like that.)

So Senhor Esplendido said, 'I will see the dentist

about making some gold teeth for Jacinto,' for that was the anaconda's name. There was quite a good dentist at Manaos, only I have forgotten his name, but it doesn't make any difference to the story what his name was. He had made a lot of gold fillings and some solid gold teeth for Senhor Esplendido, and when he opened his mouth it looked like the cellar at the Bank of England where they keep all the gold that they promise to pay you, if you ask for it, on the pound notes.

The only other man I ever knew who had as much gold in his mouth was a pilot on the Yukon river in Canada, which goes past Klondyke, where there is a lot of gold. So gold is very cheap there. You can get a lot of gold for an ordinary sort of thing, like a loaf of bread or a book, so that means that everything else except gold is very dear. I met this Yukon pilot in Mesopotamia. He was there during the war to pilot a ship that used to take soldiers up the river Tigris to fight against the Turks, and I was one of the soldiers he piloted up. He drank a great deal of whisky and used to swear wonderfully.

Well, the dentist didn't very much like the job of making teeth for an anaconda, because, as he said, 'If I am doing something to a man, however much I hurt him, he won't eat me; but a big snake like that might, or if it didn't it might squash me in its coils.'

So Senhor Esplendido said, 'Come and look at the snake to see what size and shape to make the teeth, and we will take good care he doesn't bite you when the time comes to put them in.'

They argued for a time, and then the dentist said he would do the job if he were paid three times as much as if the snake were a man. So he came in one of the swanky motor-boats and had a look at the snake's teeth. Then he went home and made some gold ones. Meanwhile Pedro Rodriguez thought of a trick to keep the snake quiet while the dentist put in the gold teeth.

Jacinto was eighteen feet long, so he got an iron drainpipe about that length, and over one end of it he fixed a cloth. In the cloth there was a round hole that could be shut up by pulling a string, like the mouth of a sponge bag. The other end was open.

Now Jacinto and his wife lived in a pen. He didn't have to live indoors like the snakes in the Zoo, because Brazil is so much warmer than London. In England you have to keep snakes in a warm place, because they don't warm themselves from inside like people and dogs and horses and birds.

Pedro made a hole in the wall of this pen and put the open end of the pipe against it. Then he got a guinea-pig, of which there are lots in Brazil, because that is one of the countries where they grow wild. He held on to Mrs Jacinto, and put the guinea-pig in the pen. It was very frightened and ran into the pipe. Jacinto crawled in after it, so it ran out at the other end, and got right away, and lived happily ever after.

Jacinto chased it, and the moment he put his head out someone pulled the string tight round his neck, so only his head was left sticking out. Then they lifted up the pipe, snake and all, and blocked up the hole in the wall so that his wife couldn't get out.

It took four men to carry him in his pipe. You can see them in the picture. Jacinto is putting his tongue out

129

because he is so angry, and hissing like anything; only the man who drew the picture didn't know how to draw a hiss, so you can't see it. The man in front is Pedro, and Senhor Esplendido and his wife are watching.

They got Jacinto in his pipe on to the motor-boat and took him to the dentist. The dentist was rather frightened, but he drank a glass of rum and got to work. First they put the pipe on a table so that Jacinto's head just stuck over the edge. Then they put another guinea-pig just in front of his mouth, and when he opened it to snap, Pedro put a stick between his jaws from the side, and he and another man held it tight while the dentist was working.

So poor Jacinto couldn't shut his mouth or turn his head round. Then the dentist got to work with his buzzer, and you should have heard Jacinto hiss. It was like a steam locomotive that has waited too long in a station, so the driver has to let some steam out or the boiler will burst.

The dentist was so frightened that he had to take another drink. However, in the end the two golden teeth were stuck in quite firmly, and they took Jacinto back to his pen and let him loose. So Senhor Esplendido was very proud, and took his wife and all his friends to see the snake with the gold teeth.

Neither Jacinto nor his wife was pleased, because they didn't think gold was any better than any other kind of stuff. That is one of the few things that snakes are more sensible about than men. I think people waste an awful lot of time and trouble making mines for gold; and when they have got it, it isn't really as useful as iron, or chocolate, or india-rubber, and not as pretty as glass, or flowers, or pictures.

Now Pedro knew what was bound to happen next, even if you don't. One day Senhor Esplendido came along to look at Jacinto, and one of the gold teeth was missing, and there was an ordinary tooth where it had been.

He lost his temper and rushed at Pedro with his big stick, shouting, 'You wicked thief, you've taken out the gold tooth and put in an ordinary false one. I'll give you the sack and have you put in prison.'

Now snakes' teeth aren't like people's. A person can grow two teeth in some places and only one in others. They lose the first lot when they are about six or seven, and if they lose the grown-up set they have to buy false ones, so it is better to get holes in them stopped before they get so bad that they have to be pulled out.

A very few extraordinary and special people can grow a third tooth where one of the grown-up ones has been pulled out. My wife did. But snakes and lizards and crocodiles can grow any number of teeth in the same place, and when one falls out another comes up. Pedro knew that; in fact, he had got a lot of Rosa's old teeth and made them into a necklace for his wife.

So he knew that Jacinto had just dropped the stump of the old tooth with the gold part stuck on it, and it must be lying about somewhere in his pen. He would have gone to look for it, only after his visit to the dentist Jacinto was so grumpy that Pedro didn't dare to go crawling about on his hands and knees for fear Jacinto would come up behind and bite his feet. For he was too poor to be able to afford boots.

Well, Pedro had thought what to do if his master went for him with a stick. He ran into the yard where the crocodile pond was and shouted for Rosa. Rosa came scuttling out of the water and sat up on her hind legs. Senhor Esplendido came after Pedro with his big stick and Pedro kept dodging round and round Rosa.

As Senhor Esplendido was running between Rosa and the pond, Rosa got angry with him for chasing her friend, and she opened her mouth very wide and made the noise an angry crocodile makes. It is something between a hiss and a snort and a bark and a grunt.

If you are lucky you can get one of the keepers at the Zoo to poke a crocodile, and then it will make that noise. But you mustn't poke it yourself for two reasons. First, you might fall into the crocodiles' tank from leaning too far over the railings.* And second, if the keeper caught you poking crocodiles you would be turned out of the Zoo and never allowed in again, which is a dreadful thing even to think of, though I suppose not so bad as being eaten by crocodiles.

But Rosa was twenty feet long, nearly twice as long as the big crocodiles at the Zoo, and twice as thick, too. The noise she made was a perfectly awful noise, and her mouth with all its teeth looked as large as a doorway. Senhor Esplendido was so frightened that he lost his balance and fell into the pond.

And Joao was waiting near the edge with his mouth open because he thought it was his feeding time. And so it was, though no one had meant it to be, for he ate

* Since I wrote this story they have put up a wire screen at the Zoo between the people and the crocodiles, so now you can't tumble in even if you want to.

Senhor Esplendido so quickly that he burnt his tongue on a cigar the Senhor was smoking. One often burns one's tongue if one eats too quickly, and I think it serves one right.

But he left one leg for Rosa, because she would have smacked him with her tail if he hadn't. So that was the end of Senhor Esplendido. And nobody knows how long his gold watch went on ticking inside Joao, because Joao went to sleep in the middle of the pond, and if you know anyone who is brave enough to swim into the middle of a pond full of man-eating crocodiles and put his ear on one of their stomachs to listen for a watch, I should like to meet him, that's all.

Well, they arrested Pedro and took him before a judge, but when the judge heard his story, he said, 'I

think it served Senhor Esplendido right, and it really wasn't your fault, so I'll let you off.'

And next week an American called Mr Fysh who was there bought Rosa off Senhor Esplendido's widow, and hired Pedro to be her keeper. And now they act together in a circus, and Rosa has learned two more tricks. She can smoke a pipe and beat time to a tune with her tail. And Pedro gets paid fifteen times as much as Senhor Esplendido used to pay him. So if that circus ever comes to England you mustn't forget to go and see it.

My Magic Collar Stud

I suppose you think there aren't any more fairies nowadays, or witches or wizards or goblins. Well, of course they don't go about dressed up like the ones in picture books. You don't see little fairies with butterfly wings perching on the chimneys at Hendon, or old ladies in pointed hats riding down Oxford Street on broomsticks and waiting for the green lights to go on. But they're doing other things. The good magicians are still doing magic things like radio and chemistry. When you're ill the doctor comes and writes a prescription on a bit of paper, and then the chemist gives you something in a bottle. If it does you good, that means that the bit of paper was really a spell, and the medicine a potion. And you meet fairies in all sorts of places, looking like quite ordinary people.

I expect you want to ask me 'How do you know they are fairies?' Well, I'll tell you. I can sometimes spot fairies and other magic people because I am descended from a fairy called Melusine. She married the Count Raymondin of Lusignan about eight hundred years ago, and they had ten children, all boys. All the kings of England after Henry II are descended from Melusine. King Henry II and his sons Richard I and John had the most awful tempers. And people in their time said it was because they were descended from a fairy. When Henry got angry he used to tear up his bedclothes with his teeth, but he was a jolly good king when he kept his temper. King George and I are both descended from Henry II, but he got the crown and I got the temper. Of course my temper is not quite as bad as King Henry's. You can't expect a temper to last seven hundred years without some of its corners getting rubbed a bit. And the king has a better crown than King Henry had, because since King Henry's time people have dug up a lot of diamonds and put them in the crown, as you can see if you go to the Tower of London.

By the way, I forgot to tell you that Melusine became a snake from the waist downwards every Saturday. If you want to know more you can read a book about her that my wife wrote.

The last fairy I met lives in Wandsworth, and keeps a magic shop there. In the window of the magic shop you always see a lot of different kinds of things, such as pen-knives and sweets and pails, and capstan bars and scales and weights and ornaments for empty grates, as the poet says. You hardly ever find a fairy keeping shop with only one sort of thing, like a greengrocer's or a tailor's or a fishmonger's. And of course fairies *never* keep large shops because you can't trust other people to sell magic things. They sell them to the wrong sorts of people. I mean what earthly use would a pair of seven-league boots be to a bus driver? And yet they're just what a postman needs. Or think what would happen if someone sold a cloak of darkness or a cap of invisibility to a traffic policeman. He'd be invisible and all the cars and lorries and buses would run over him. Besides no one would see him holding his hand up. But of course a cap of invisibility is awfully useful to a window cleaner because he can clean the windows without stopping any of the light. And it's very useful to a man in a big tailor's shop. He just makes himself invisible and moves the dummy ladies and gentlemen in the window about. And then everyone stops and says, 'What a clever machine,' and some of them come in and buy new hats and trousers and skirts and waistcoats and things.

I went into this shop because it looked rather magic to me, and I wanted a new stud, because I had lost the one I had before in the front of my shirt, so I had to fix my collar on to my shirt with a paper-clip, and the ends of it were sharp and ran into my neck. There was a nice-looking lady behind the counter. She had rather grey hair, but no wrinkles on her face as you'd expect to find with grey hair. I told her I wanted a stud because I had lost my old one.

'Is that all you've lost?' she asked.

'Well, no,' I said, 'as a matter of fact, I lost my temper too.'

'Oh dear,' she replied, 'I hope it wasn't a valuable temper. What do you do when you lose your temper? Some people put an advertisement in the paper, "Lost, on Friday, August 28th, in Old Kent Road, one pink temper with orange and purple spots. Answers to the name of Bisclaveret. Finder will be rewarded with a full set of butterfly cigarette cards or a set of bound volumes of the *Radio Times*." Of course Roman Catholics burn a candle to St Anthony like they do when they lose anything else. And some people go to the Lost Tempers'

Home in Battersea, but they often can't recognize their temper among such a lot of others.'

'I think I should recognize mine, because it is quite a special one, about eight hundred years old. It belonged to a lady called Melusine. Of course it's rather dented in places, but it's a real temper, not like those wretched squeaky little things they grow nowadays.'

'Did you buy it in an antique shop?'

'Oh no, it's a family heirloom.'

'Well, I'm delighted to meet any descendant of Melusine. I knew her quite well, and I should hate to think of a temper that had belonged to her getting lost. Though of course it isn't so odd really. She had a son called Geoffrey Grossdent (which means Bigtooth), and he lost his so often that in the end they had to put a collar round its neck and take it round on a leash. I might be able to do that for you if you need it, but meanwhile let's see about the stud. I've got all sorts. Here's a tray of invisible ones.'

She held out what looked like an empty tray.

'Thank you so much, but I don't know if I could find it in the morning, and besides, an invisible collar stud isn't really much use unless you and your clothes are invisible too. Of course you want one then. It would never do to see a collar stud all alone going along the street in the air.'

'Well, I suppose you'd better have an Unlosable then. That'll be fourpence three farthings.'

It was lucky that I had four pennies and three farthings. Because of course fairies are very particular about that sort of thing. I mean if I'd offered her a halfpenny and a farthing instead of the three farthings I should think the shop would have vanished and I would have found myself talking to a statue of Mr Gladstone. And anyone who asks a fairy for change is lucky if he isn't turned into anything worse than an automatic machine for selling cigarettes. After being one of them for a year or two you'd understand why fairies don't like giving change either.

But if you're not the sort of person who carries farthings about you'd better not go into a fairy shop at all. Most boys and girls do carry farthings. But when they grow up they think farthings are silly. That's all wrong, of course, because farthings are the very magi-cest sort of money there is in England, except silver pennies, which nobody's made for hundreds of years.

Well, I got my stud, and I've got it still. And I suppose it will be buried with me when I die, because if they don't put it in my coffin it will come hopping after the hearse all down the road, and all the people who ought to be crying will laugh. I've tried to lose that stud three or four times. Once I threw it down a grating in the gutter during a thunderstorm when there was a lot of water to wash it away. About half an hour later I was washing my hands when it popped up out of the sink, all wet, and started fighting with another stud I had put in its place. Between them they nearly made a hole in my neck.

Once when I was in South Africa an ostrich ate it, and I thought it was gone. But next morning I found it in my egg at breakfast, which I was sharing with two other men and a dog. That's one of the advantages of ostriches over hens. One egg makes a meal for the whole family. Another time it fell out of a porthole in the middle of the Atlantic ocean when the steward was folding up my clothes. I suppose you think I'm going to tell you I found the stud in a fish I was eating at dinner, like King Polycrates' ring. But you're wrong. I got it back a lot quicker than that. You know the thing like a tin fish on a line that they tow behind ships to tell them how far they've gone in a day. It's called the log, and twiddles round and round in the water. That twists the cord, and the cord turns a thing like a clock on the ship, so that the captain and sailors can see how far she has gone in an hour or a day. Well, suddenly the cord stopped twisting, so they knew something was wrong with the log, because the ship hadn't stopped. They pulled it in, and found it all tangled up with a cuttlefish which was holding on to it with nine of its arms, and my stud was stuck on to a sucker on its tenth.

But there were about a thousand passengers on the ship and nothing written on the stud to say it was mine. So I'd never have got it, if it hadn't been that five minutes later a steward came into my cabin and asked me to come and see a cuttlefish that had just been caught. I'm not a professor of zoology, but there was one on the ship, and the captain had mixed him up with me, and thought I could tell him the Latin name of the cuttlefish, which I couldn't. But I found my stud.

It was after that that I started trying to lose it for fun. Once I was motoring along a narrow road and saw a notice 'Steam-roller at work', so I slowed down. Of course if I saw a notice 'Steam-roller at play' I should run away quickly, because a playful steam-roller might tread on my foot just for fun, and then I should be flat-footed. If a steam-roller goes over anything it leaves it flat. And yesterday I read an advertisement in the newspaper about a man who said he could cure flat feet. So I suppose you go to him if a steam-roller treads on your toe. But this steam-roller was working quite hard, and I had to stop the car. I thought just for fun I would see what happened if I threw my stud under the steam-roller. But I wish I hadn't. Because when the big front wheel went over it, instead of the stud being squashed, the wheel just cracked in two with the most fearful bang. The driver was awfully angry, for he was very fond of his steam-roller. I said I'd pay for a new wheel, because it was really my fault. But the man who made the steam-roller wouldn't let me, because he said if I did everyone would laugh at him, and say, 'Don't buy Smith's steam-rollers. They can't even squash a collar stud.'

Once I gave the stud away to a clergyman who had been very kind to me. Of course you know that a clergyman wears his collar the wrong way round, so he has a back stud at the front and a front stud at the back. Well, about two hours after I gave it to him he was reading a verse in the Bible that says, 'The first shall be last, and the last first,' when suddenly he felt his collar turn right round so as to have the opening in front like an ordinary man's. So he just said, 'This stud's much too clever for me. I want a stud that stays where it's put.' And he sent me the stud back. So now I expect I shall keep it till I die, and perhaps after.

Oh dear! I've been telling you about all sorts of things that happened long after I left that shop. I wish I were like those clever people who write long stories with all the things in the same order that they happened. I just tell you them as they come into my head.

After I had bought the stud I asked the lady behind the counter what her name was, because I thought if she had known Melusine who was my very, very great grandmother she must be quite an old lady, and have seen some interesting things. 'You can call me Miss Wandle,' she said, 'though I had to wait a good many

thousand years before I had a name at all, and I've had
two or three others in my time. I used to live in the
river, but it's got too dirty in the last century. I expect
I shall go back there again fairly soon. I don't suppose
there'll be much of London left in another two or three
thousand years.'

'It's very kind of you to keep a shop where one can
get such really useful things.'

'Oh I've always given things to the right sort of
people. They used to come to me when I lived in the
river. Eight hundred years ago they called me a fairy,
and before that the Romans called me a naiad, and the
bronze-age people, who were really much the nicest lot
there've ever been in England, called me a wasi. But I
can't be as helpful now as I used to be. I remember there
was a most fearful dragon who lived up on Wimbledon
Common. All sorts of knights tried to kill him, but it
was no good. He breathed fire at them and it went
through their armour like a burglar's blowpipe goes
through a tin can. One day he chased one right into
the Wandle with his armour red-hot.

'It fizzled like anything. Luckily I was there and
pulled the knight out after he had cooled down a bit.
Then I ticked him off properly. I asked him how he
was going to kill a magic beast like a dragon with an
ordinary spear and armour. So next week he took on
the dragon wearing an asbestos suit and carrying two
fire extinguishers instead of a spear. And that was the
end of the dragon. The first fire extinguisher put out the
flame in his mouth, and the second killed him. Of course
in those days there weren't any ordinary fire extinguish-

ers, but only magic ones. The knight was awfully grateful and planted a lot of flowering rushes along my bank in some places where it was rather bare, besides some lovely weeping willows.

'But they're all gone now. That's what's made my hair grey. But I expect the colour will come back again one day. Still I suppose I ought to be thankful my river hasn't been put in a pipe like the West Bourne. You can see the pipe going over the railway at Sloane Square Station. You men do make an awful mess. But I've no right to talk when I think of the mess I made in my young days. About forty thousand years ago it was so cold that a glacier came as near as Muswell Hill, and even round here there was ice for most of the year. When things got a bit warmer and the ice melted, the rivers *were* rivers. Why, the Wandle was sometimes nearly as big as the Thames is now. And the mud we carried down was something fearful. Yes, I've made a mess in my time.

'Is there anything else I can show you this afternoon? I've got a very nice line in magic mangles. And you might care to try some magic bootlaces. But of course they may be a trouble.'

I certainly didn't want any magic bootlaces, because I once knew a man called MacFarlane who bought a pair. They were awfully useful of course, and never came untied. But one day he forgot the spell to loosen them, so he had to go to bed in his boots for three months until he met a wizard who knew the right word. Then he wrote it down in his pocket-book and had no more trouble that way. But the boots got rather worn, and one day his wife sent them to the bootmaker to be re-soled. The laces didn't like being sent to an ordinary shop, so they wriggled out of the boots and started to find their way home. All sorts of people saw them crawling along the street and tried to catch them. Of course they couldn't, but they chased them into Mr MacFarlane's front garden and trampled down all his flowers in the hunt. And when the laces got into the house the cook thought they were snakes, and gave notice. No wonder I thought I'd sooner have ordinary laces, even if they do sometimes break.

So I thanked Miss Wandle very much, and went away with my magic collar stud.

There are now more than 500 Puffins in print, and some of them are described on the following pages.

Half Magic

Edward Eager

It happened to four children in an American city called
Toledo, one summer's day about thirty years ago. The day
began particularly well, with a glint of something metal in the
pavement. 'Ooh, a lucky nickel,' Jane said, and scooped it into
her pocket. She would get round to thinking about spending
it later, after the adventures of the morning.

But the adventures didn't come, and they couldn't think of
anything exciting to do. Jane was so disgusted that she said
right out loud she wished there'd be a fire. The other three
looked shocked at such wickedness, but they looked more
shocked a minute later. For what they heard next was a fire-
engine.

The Borrowers

Mary Norton

The Borrowers lived in the secret places of quiet old houses:
behind the mantelpiece, inside the harpsichord, under the
kitchen clock. They owned nothing, borrowed everything, and
thought human beings were invented just to do the dirty
work – great slaves put there for them to use.

Arrietty's father, Pod, was an expert borrower. He could
scale curtains using a hat-pin, and bring back a doll's teacup
without breaking it. Girls weren't supposed to go borrowing,
but as Arrietty was an only child her father broke the rule,
and then something happened which changed their lives. She
made friends with the Boy.

Joe and the Gladiator

Catherine Cookson

How do you manage to look after a horse if you have no home or money? This was the problem that faced Joe Darling when his old friend Mr Prodhurst bequeathed to him The Gladiator, the ancient, intelligent horse which had once pulled a rag-and-bone cart.

But it was a challenge he had to meet, and by sheer determination and with the help of some very surprising friends, he managed to keep the old horse and his efforts were rewarded in ways neither he nor his family would ever have guessed.

This story, which has been dramatised for television, will be enjoyed by readers of nine and over.

I am David

Anne Holm

David lay quite still in the darkness of the concentration camp, waiting for the signal. 'You must get away tonight,' the man had told him. 'Stay awake so that you're ready just before the guard is changed. When you see me strike a match, the current will be cut off and you can climb over – you'll have half a minute, no more. Follow the compass southwards till you get to Salonica and then find a ship that's bound for Italy, and then go north till you come to a country called Denmark – you'll be safe there.'

So David, who had known no other life but that of the concentration camp, escaped into a world he knew nothing of, not even what things to eat nor how to tell good men from bad.

A deeply moving story, highly recommended for readers of 11 and over.

The Dribblesome Teapots and Other Incredible Stories

Norman Hunter

'Oh, oh, oh, oh! This is terrible,' cried the Queen. 'Not a teapot in the Palace that can be used. Oh, disgraceful! I must have a teapot that doesn't dribble, I must! I must! Half the kingdom as a reward for anyone who can bring me a teapot that pours without dribbling!'

'Here, here, half a mo!' cried the King, getting all agitated. 'You can't do that. What do you think's going to happen to Sypso-Sweetleigh if you go offering half of it for teapots?' But it was too late, the Royal Herald had shouted the proclamation all round the city.

By the author of *Professor Branestawm*, this is a marvellous collection of outrageous fairy tales, where the characters struggle against problems that are not nearly as simple as the old legends suggest.

The Starlight Barking

Dodie Smith

Pongo and Missis, the famous pair in *The Hundred and One Dalmatians*, wake up one morning to discover that every living thing is in a deep sleep – except the dogs. And this is only the beginning of some very strange happenings.

Ghostly Gallery

Alfred Hitchcock

Eleven weird and uncanny ghost stories collected by Alfred Hitchcock, the master of mystery. They include really spooky spinechilling stories, some fanciful ones, and some in which the phantoms and apparitions are even treated humorously. Some of the phantoms are true shades of darkness, and others, stranger still, appear in the glare of the sun at noon or deep in the forest shadows – you may see a spook any day of your life.

For fearless readers of ten upwards.

How To Be Topp

Geoffrey Willans and Ronald Searle

It is only fair to admit that Nigel Molesworth, the Curse of St Custards, is not everybody's favourite character. There are masters who ban his presence in the school library, or cite him as an Awful Warning to their pupils, and there are parents who condemn his manners and his spelling as a disgrace to the noble name of Education. But there are also parents, the kind who treasure their children's first letters, who find him irresistible, and masters who use him as a valuable guide in the strange labyrinth of a Schoolboy's Mind.

A book for everyone over nine who wants to laugh and knows how to spell.

Saturday and the Irish Aunt

Jenifer Wayne

Jessica, Nonnie and Ben had never met their grandfather
while he was alive, and certainly didn't expect his will to be
interesting – but they were wrong, for he had left each of them
fifty pounds, *to spend exactly as they liked*.

Fifty pounds each! It was odd that in spite of their
excitement they could think of so few practical ways of
spending it that were neither too big nor too small. Jessica
was bursting with schemes, like starting a pottery or building
a theatre, and Ben was torn between ideas of modernising his
bedroom, motorbikes, and buying a cow. And Nonnie? She
was in the worst dilemma of all, she had to choose between
the lovely pony she longed to buy and saving grandfather's
poor old mare in Ireland.

And then, as if the excitement wasn't already at boiling
point, their Irish Aunt arrived.

For readers of nine and over.

Catweazle

Richard Carpenter

Catweazle was a magician who lived in the 11th century, but
usually his spells didn't work. But one day was different, and
he flew through Time instead of Space, and ended up on a
place called Hexwood Farm nine centuries later, where of
course he thought everything he saw – motor cars, telephones,
electric light ('Eleck-trickery') – all happened by magic.

How Catweazle is befriended by the farmer's son Carrot, and
how he finds his feet in the 20th century, while hiding from the
world in a water tower, makes a riotously funny story, as
anyone who has seen the television serial will know.

For readers of eight and over.

If you have enjoyed this book and would like to know about others which we publish, why not join the Puffin Club? You will be sent the Club magazine *Puffin Post* four times a year and a smart badge and membership book. You will also be able to enter all the competitions.

For details send a stamped addressed envelope to:
The Puffin Club Dept A
Penguin Books
Bath Road
Harmondsworth
Middlesex